"You're going to be difficult, aren't you?"

Brad caught her skeptical look. "Difficult and stubborn," he continued, "but that's all right. That's one of the things I like about you."

She sighed. "I'm not sure I know what you're talking about now, Brad."

"You will, Harriet, in time...."

She gave a nervous laugh. "You sound as if this could take all night."

"Oh, it will," he said matter-of-factly. "Definitely. I've decided it's futile to continue any discussion about your character until I've got a little something out of the way."

A prickle ran up and down her spine. "A little something? What little something?"

"Your virginity, Harriet."

MIRANDA LEE was born and brought up in New South Wales, Australia. She had a brief career as cellist in an orchestra, and then another as a computer programmer. A move to the country after marriage and the birth of the first of three daughters limited her career opportunities to being a full-time wife and mother. Encouraged by her family, she began writing in 1982. She favors a well-paced what-happens-next kind of story, but says what matters most "is that my books please and entertain my readers, leaving them feeling good and optimistic about love and marriage in our present topsy-turvy world."

Books by Miranda Lee

MIRANDA LEE

Scandalous Seduction

Harlequin Books

TORONTO • NEW YORK • LONDON
AMSTERDAM • PARIS • SYDNEY • HAMBURG
STOCKHOLM • ATHENS • TOKYO • MILAN
MADRID • WARSAW • BUDAPEST • AUCKLAND

Harlequin Presents first edition September 1993
ISBN 0-373-11589-X

Original hardcover edition published in 1991
by Mills & Boon Limited

SCANDALOUS SEDUCTION

CHAPTER ONE

HARRIET'S eyes snapped up to stare at her mother. '*Who* did you say?'

Julia Weatherspoon raised her finely arched eyebrows towards the ceiling. 'I'm so glad to have finally gained your full attention, Harriet. Truly, once you get your nose into one of those infernal books of yours!'

'Sorry...' Harriet closed the battered copy of *Wuthering Heights* and gave her mother a soothing smile. 'Come on, don't make me suffer. Was I right or was I wrong in thinking you just mentioned Brad Barrington?'

Her mother sighed. 'I suppose you haven't heard more than those two words, have you?'

'*Mo-ther!*'

'All right, all right, yes, I did say Brad Barrington and, yes, I mean the famous author. I doubt there are many men named Brad Barrington in Australia.'

'Well, what about him?' Harriet urged impatiently.

Her mother's glare was full of reproach. 'You haven't been listening at all, have you? Good heavens, Harriet, you really are the limit sometimes. There's more to life than reading. I've spent at least ten minutes telling you how your father's mystery buyer for that awful commune place on Mist Mountain has turned out to be none other than our aforesaid celebrity author.'

'Well, that's wonderful, Mother, but not so astonishing. It's not the first time a millionaire has bought land around these hills.'

'Yes, but he's going to *live* here!'

Harriet's big brown eyes opened wide. '*Live* here?'

'He moved in yesterday, it seems. Raymond rang me earlier to tell me Mr Barrington had just dropped in to his office to say how delighted he was with the place. And you know your father. He upped and asked him to dinner tonight. That's what I was telling you a moment ago.'

Harriet blinked. 'Father asked Brad Barrington to dinner? Tonight?' She swallowed convulsively. 'And is he coming?'

'He is.' Julia smoothed her still-beautiful face into a superbly bland expression, as though it were perfectly normal for her to have fabulously rich and famous dinner guests. In truth, she was a splendid hostess, and her dinner invitations were prized among the locals, but even Harriet could see that this would be a feather in her cap.

Brad Barrington... Harriet's heart gave a definite leap. She had seen him interviewed on television recently about his new release, and, while she couldn't recall the name of the book, she *could* recall her involuntary reaction to the man who had written it. She'd found herself glued to the set, watching him with increasing fascination as he sparred with the interviewer.

It wasn't that he was overly handsome. Attractive covered his looks best. It was his mind that had captured her interest. So quick, so intelligent, with a no-nonsense attitude to life that had really appealed to her. He had called a spade a spade, not bothering to dress up his answers with a lot of insincere social affectations.

And yet he had sufficient magnetism and charisma—plus a bagful of captivating smiles—to make his rather blunt answers not sound rude. They had been frank and refreshing, despite the cynicism that flavoured their delivery.

When the woman interviewer had dared to ask him why a man of his obvious literary talent continued to write the sex and spice type of novel, instead of something *worthwhile*, Brad Barrington had lifted a supercilious eyebrow, then smiled drily.

'My dear lady,' he'd returned, 'I wrote serious novels for ten years. The manuscripts are still lying in a drawer because no publisher would touch them. One can starve writing unpublished masterpieces. So now I write what the people want. And do you know what? It's damned hard writing what the people want. Damned hard... It pays well, though,' he had finished with a winning grin.

Did it ever! He had reportedly received two million dollars for the television rights to *Seduction* and was supposedly negotiating for more for *Corruption*. Though Harriet's mind boggled at how they would make films out of his stories. Heavens, the film would melt!

But, to be truthful, she had privately agreed with the interviewer. It did seem a shame that a man of his writing ability didn't attempt a novel of more depth and magnitude. She didn't doubt that his bestsellers were hard to write, and she had enjoyed them herself in an escapist fashion, but she couldn't imagine anyone reading any of his novels more than once, or ever studying them. Yes, in a way Brad Barrington *had* prostituted his talent for money. Not an altogether admirable trait.

Yet she had been intrigued by the man. He had stayed in her mind for days afterwards. And he was coming here...to her home...for dinner...tonight.

'I was thinking,' her mother added carefully, 'that you and Mr Barrington might hit it off. I mean...well...'

A warning bell went off in Harriet's head and she slanted an apprehensive look her mother's way. Finding a husband for her elder daughter was Julia Weatherspoon's favourite occupation.

Harriet's stomach twisted. She wished her mother would let well enough alone. It wasn't that Harriet wasn't interested in marrying. She was. She liked men. And she had recovered—in a fashion—from the crippling blow Amanda and Graham had dealt her. After all, four years had gone by and it was impossible to remain devastated forever, even if your younger sister *had* run off with your fiancé.

But couldn't her mother see that the problem lay in something Harriet had no control over? She just wasn't the sort of woman most men found sexually appealing. That was the simple truth of the matter.

'I hope you don't seriously think a man like Brad Barrington would be interested in me?' she said firmly.

Julia fairly bristled. 'And why not, pray tell? You're an attractive and charming woman.'

Harriet sighed. *Attractive and charming?* Did all mothers exaggerate their daughters' attributes?

'Mr Barrington already has a lady-friend,' she explained calmly, knowing that this was one tack her mother couldn't refute. 'A certain Miss Lydia Richmond, television newsreader *extraordinaire*.' Their affair had been a hot gossip item in the papers and magazines for ages.

'Oh, *her*,' Julia tossed off. 'She's no problem. Mr Barrington told Raymond they'd split up. Permanently.'

Harriet shook her head in wonderment. But she didn't doubt it. People seemed to tell her father everything. He had a salesman's way with him, making prospective clients talk and tell him things they wouldn't normally. The folk around town used to say that Harriet had inherited her father's intelligence and gift of the gab; Amanda, her mother's grace and beauty. Sometimes Harriet felt she had got the better deal. But not tonight. No...definitely not tonight.

'Now, Harriet,' her mother was saying. 'I know what you're thinking. That interfering mother of mine is at it again, and you're right! But Mr Barrington seems eminently suitable husband material for you. He's obviously grown tired of the fast city life. *And* fast city women, I don't doubt. He probably wants peace and quiet, and a woman by his side who will appreciate and understand his work. Someone like you...'

When Harriet went to protest that a thirty-six-year-old bachelor was likely to remain one, her mother hushed her with a look. 'At twenty-six you're not getting any younger, my dear, and I know that underneath you still want to get married. I also know you wouldn't want to marry any old man. Now let's face it, how many times does an attractive, well-educated, wealthy, unattached gentleman come to live near our town? I mean, Valley's End isn't exactly the ends of the earth, but . . . well . . .' Her voice trailed away tellingly.

Harriet was forced to concede that her home town was hardly a thriving metropolis, tucked away as it was in a valley in the Northern Tablelands of New South Wales. Though the town's relative proximity to the coastline and the booming tourist trade there had brought some rewards for the local property industry in recent months.

Several large tracts of land in the hills around Valley's End had already been snapped up, with the townsfolk hoping that the owners might be rich millionaires intent on building luxury hideaways—anything to inject a bit of money into the fading town. Valley's End had once serviced a huge sugar-cane and banana growing area but with the plummeting prices of both commodities the once buoyant economy was past history.

But the millionaires had so far failed to materialise in person, the properties having clearly been bought as long-range investments. Except, it seemed, for Mist Mountain, and the one and only Brad Barrington!

Harriet frowned. It did seem out of character for such a man to buy a remote mountain retreat to live on. In his television interview he'd revealed that he thrived on his jet-setting city life, writing his novels in a penthouse unit in King's Cross in Sydney, where he could soak up the cosmopolitan atmosphere for his fast-paced novels. He had openly spurned the cliché of burying himself in a log cabin in order to write, vowing he needed noise and 'colourful' people around him for inspiration.

What had changed all that? His break-up with Lydia Richmond perhaps?

'What if I don't like him?' Harriet pointed out quite sensibly.

Her mother's lovely blue eyes opened with genuine astonishment. 'But of course you'll like him. How could you not like a man so rich and clever? Besides, you have so much in common, both of you being writers.'

Harriet thought of the play she'd been working on for years and chuckled wryly. 'I'm not a writer, Mother. I'm a high school English teacher who dabbles in writing as a hobby.'

'Just because you haven't been published doesn't mean you're not a writer. You write beautifully.'

Harriet smiled to herself, knowing that to tell her mother that all her manoeuvrings were a waste of time would be futile. She didn't understand the word. 'At least promise me you won't say anything embarrassing in front of Mr Barrington tonight,' Harriet insisted.

Julia raised her eyebrows. '*Me?* Say something *embarrassing*? I'd watch my own tongue, if I were you, my girl. Sometimes you say the most tactless things.'

Harriet was taken aback. And showed it.

'It's not that you *mean* to be rude,' her mother hastened to explain. 'But remember when I asked Mrs Gallagher's nephew to dinner? And you made it quite clear you knew he had only come back to Valley's End because he thought the old lady was going to die and he wanted to make sure of his inheritance? The poor man didn't know where to look. It's no wonder he didn't call back.'

'But Mother, he hadn't been near that sweet old lady for years! Where was he when she had that nasty operation on her hip a year ago, I ask you?'

'People aren't perfect, Harriet. Some girls just can't afford to be so picky!' Julia flushed when she realised she might have betrayed that she didn't believe her daughter to be quite as charming and attractive as she had asserted earlier. 'Oh, my goodness, look at the time. I'll have to get the roast on.' She jumped up and hurried towards the kitchen. 'Now make sure you wear an especially pretty dress tonight, Harriet,' she threw over her shoulder. 'We want Mr Barrington to see you at your best.'

Harriet watched her mother's hasty departure with exasperation. My best, Mother dear, she thought ruefully, will fall far short of what is required to attract the likes of our famous visitor.

A light laugh bubbled up from her throat. Good heavens! What did it matter if Brad Barrington liked her or not? She was beginning to let her mother's plottings get to her. As if marriage were the be-all and end-all, anyway.

Harriet was happy with her life at the moment. Quite happy. She had returned home from Sydney to live this year and was thoroughly enjoying teaching in a country high school, a welcome change after the stress of handling city kids. Yes...life was quite good at the moment.

Nevertheless, when she returned to her bedroom she set about making the most of herself, telling her grumbling conscience that it was merely her pride that was insisting on such a vast effort.

*   *   *

Harriet stood back from her dressing-table mirror for a final assessment.

Not too bad, actually, she decided.

In the last couple of years she had finally come to terms with her looks, and in doing so had achieved a certain style of her own.

Gone were the frilly feminine dresses her mother had selected for her as a girl. Her present wardrobe was filled exclusively with tailored clothes which gave an elegance to her tall, slender frame, her long-legged, boyish figure looking particularly good in straight slim skirts and well-cut trousers.

Her hair too had undergone a drastic change from the lank mop that had used to stretch halfway down her back, and resisted curling no matter what torture it was subjected to. She now sported an excellently cut blunt bob, the straight thick brown hair swinging around her jawline, softening the sharp edges of her face. The top Sydney hairdresser who had achieved this miracle had suggested a layered fringe as well, showing how it disguised her high forehead.

Nothing, however, could disguise the thinness of her oval face, which made her cheekbones stand out and the widely set brown eyes seem enormous. Still, Harriet admitted that the fringe had minimised the doe-eyed effect somewhat, giving the eyes shadows which a romantic might have called mysterious.

A romantic...

Harriet conceded that no one would call her that. Life had taught her to be cruelly honest with herself. When she looked in the mirror she saw only a moderately attractive young woman who for some reason did not appeal to men on any level except a platonic one.

It had always been like that. In her years at school she'd had several friends who were boys, yet no boyfriends. At university, the other male students had often sought her out to talk to, to study with. They had seemed to enjoy probing her mind, but never her body.

And yet she had been a normal girl, with a normal girl's desires. She had thought about romance and sex as much, if not *more* than some of her girlfriends.

By the age of twenty-two, and doing her Diploma of Education, she had begun to think that she would never have a boyfriend, never be made love to. Then Graham had come into her life.

He had been her tutor, doing his doctorate in literature, an aesthetically handsome young man who had had all the female students swooning. Being top of the class, Harriet had attracted his interest at first in an intellectual way, and they'd begun going for coffee after lectures, then to the occasional movie. By the time he kissed her, several weeks later, Harriet had been deeply, irrevocably in love.

It amazed her now that Graham had ever asked her to marry him, for she could see with hindsight that he had never been in love with her. If he had, he would have been far more anxious to go to bed with her. But it had been he who had always pulled back, he who had said he wanted to wait till they were married, that he wanted their relationship to be different from others he had had. With no pressure—whatever that had meant.

Though frustrated at the time, Harriet had thought Graham wonderfully romantic and contented herself with sweet kisses and tender words. With stars in her eyes and a ring on her finger she had brought him home from Sydney to show him off to her family. She could still recall the way Amanda had looked at him from the very first moment...

Remembered pain wrapped its cruel tentacles around Harriet's heart and squeezed, bringing an unbidden sob to her lips. She snatched up her old rag doll and hugged it fiercely. 'You love me though, don't you?' she whispered into the well-worn face.

The knocking on the door and the opening happened simultaneously. Her mother came in, her face falling when she saw what her daughter was wearing. 'But... but I thought you were going to wear a dress!'

Harriet sighed and placed the doll on the pillow. She glanced down at her clothes, a tan pair of linen trousers—superbly cut—matched with a toning striped vest and off-white blazer. Off-white flat loafers covered her surprisingly small feet. The outfit was comfortable and stylish. And suited her.

'Don't you like it?' she asked, unable to hide her hurt.

'Well, I... well, it's...' Julia was flummoxed. 'You *know* I prefer you in a dress,' she finally hedged. 'I especially wanted you to look nice tonight.'

'I think I do look nice,' Harriet said patiently. Why couldn't her mother see that what had looked good on Amanda wasn't right for her?

'But your father hates women wearing trousers, you know that.'

Harriet's smile had a touch of irony. 'Father won't notice what I wear. He's only invited Mr Barrington to dinner to make a business contact. He's hoping that maybe some other wealthy writers will want to buy retreats around here in the future. Real estate is the name of the game, Mother, not trying to marry off old-maid daughters.'

'That's not true, Harriet! Your father told me Mr Barrington expressed a particular desire to meet you.'

This widened the brown eyes. 'For heaven's sake, why?' she laughed.

Even Julia looked perplexed, which was hardly flattering. 'Well, I——'

'Never mind,' Harriet finished. 'Come along. It's time we joined Father in the living-room. He'll be like a cat on a hot tin roof waiting for his prey to arrive.'

Julia shook her head, though the carefully coiffured blonde curls on her head did not budge an inch. 'I don't think I'll ever understand you, Harriet,' she murmured as she preceded her daughter along the hallway, across the small foyer and down the steps into the sunken living-room, moving with an inbuilt elegance that Harriet had always envied. Amanda had inherited it, as well as the blonde beauty and overt sex appeal that shone out like a beacon, beckoning to any male within a hundred feet.

Raymond Weatherspoon looked up from where he was standing at the cocktail cabinet, and immediately responded to it. 'A sherry for you, darling?' he asked, moving over to kiss his wife's cheek. His gaze landed indifferently on Harriet over her shoulder. 'Oh . . . and you, Harriet, what would you like?'

'Nothing, thanks,' she said, noting wryly that she had been right. He hadn't noticed what she was wearing. He really was a most selfish man, living and breathing his property business, working nearly every weekend, giving his family only the smallest dollops of his time. And yet her mother seemed happy with him, Harriet realised, which was a puzzle. But then her mother's requirements of a husband were not as exacting as Harriet's. She would want to share *everything* with the man she married.

The chimes of the doorbell interrupted her thoughts, and brought a rush of nerves. She was about to meet Brad Barrington. And, despite her having swept aside her mother's machinations as ridiculous, he *was* an interesting man, and Harriet had been secretly flattered by his expressed desire to meet her. Why, she couldn't fathom. Perhaps her father had been talking about her writing, though she didn't think that likely.

Her father frowned and looked at his watch. 'Damn it all! The man's early. You get the door, Harriet. I have to finish mixing the cocktails.' He began walking back to the bar.

'I'll check that everything's in order in the kitchen,' Julia said. 'Oh, Ray, darling?'

Her husband stopped in his tracks, his face instantly attentive on his wife's. 'Yes?'

She gave him a dazzling smile. 'I just wanted to tell you how handsome you look tonight in your

new suit. Grey is your colour.' She blew him a kiss
and moved off, leaving him looking puffed up and
self-satisfied.

Harriet tried to stifle a surge of irritation. But
failed. She knew flattery and coyness worked with
men, having watched the strategy used to per-
fection by both her mother and Amanda. But
something inside her rebelled against such blatantly manipulative tactics. It seemed
somehow...demeaning...to both the man and
woman concerned. With an oddly sinking heart
Harriet realised that if that was the secret to a
woman's sex appeal then she was doomed forever.

'The *door*, Harriet!'

She clenched her jaw and hurried away, her long,
coltish strides carrying her quickly from the room,
but as she approached the front door nerves
crowded her stomach. She swept open the door with
her best 'How-do-you-do?' smile, only to find it
freezing on her lips as she took in her mother's
prized guest.

Shock must have swept over her face.

Brad Barrington straightened from where one
broad shoulder had been holding up a column to
stand, long legs apart, on the edge of the porch.
'The Weatherspoon residence?' came the lazily
drawled words.

Harriet's rounded eyes travelled down then up
his body in poorly concealed amazement.
Nobody—and she meant *nobody*!—had ever presented themself at her mother's house for dinner
dressed in such a disreputable fashion. The well-
worn black cords and crumpled shirt looked as if
they were rejects from a jumble sale!

Harriet's mouth gaped even further when he moved forward—all six feet three of him—into the circle of light thrown by the wall lamp.

He hadn't even *shaved*!

'Something wrong?'

Harriet's stunned gaze jerked from the stubbly chin to his eyes. An amused and decidedly intelligent light flashed in their striking blue depths, one wickedly arched eyebrow angling skywards.

Dear heaven, but he was a lot better looking in the flesh than he'd appeared on television. Perhaps he was not the photogenic type, she thought dazedly, for up close, and live, he was exuding a macho attractiveness that was overpowering, and vaguely threatening. He loomed over her, the total male animal, making her feel more vulnerably feminine than she ever had in her life.

She swallowed, and found her startled gaze lifting to his tousled hair, which was far too long but none the less sexy. In the light she could see that the wayward waves were streaked with grey, making the mid-brown colour look smoky. Yet the grey touches and the lived-in lines around his eyes and mouth somehow contrived to make him more attractive.

'Cat got your tongue, babe?'

Harriet's mouth dropped even further as she recalled that 'babe' was what the hero in *Seduction* had called every female companion he had had. And she meant *had*! Was he a semi-autobiographical figure? she wondered. If he was then it brought a different meaning to Brad Barrington's expressed wish to meet her. To our intrepid fictional hero—and maybe his creator—

wanting to meet a woman was synonymous with wanting to bed her.

Harriet found her mouth going dry with speculation, and she gathered her wits with difficulty.

'You're early, Mr Barrington,' she said with creditable composure. 'And the name's Harriet.'

'Harriet.' He grinned and slid his hands into the pockets of the disgusting cords. They were so old and baggy that they flapped around his thighs.

Her mother was going to have a pink fit when she saw him!

He leant forward slightly. 'Harriet what?'

'Weatherspoon.'

One of the arched eyebrows lifted again as he straightened, but he said nothing.

His surprise prodded at Harriet's powers of deduction, bringing a jab of dismay. So! Her father had lied about his wanting to meet her. He didn't even know there *was* a Harriet Weatherspoon. She should have known it was too good to be true!

'Are we going to wait out here until I'm on time?' he enquired cheekily.

Harriet gave him a reproving look. No doubt he tried to charm every female he came into contact with but he needn't think he could flirt with her just out of habit.

'If you will follow me,' she said coolly, turning and showing him the way into the foyer.

'Yes, ma'am.'

Harriet resisted glancing over her shoulder but she could have sworn he actually clicked his heels. Somehow she could feel him smiling at her back.

The feeling that he was mocking her wiped out any pleasurable anticipation of the evening ahead.

What a fool she had been to let her mother's talk worm its way into her subconscious. The sweet woman really had no idea of the ways of the real world outside Valley's End. Fancy ever imagining that a man like Brad Barrington could be her difficult daughter's knight in shining armour! Having met him, Harriet could see the idea was ludicrous in the extreme. He wouldn't look twice at her let alone marry her!

But knowing that this was so didn't make it any less hurtful. Harriet compressed her mouth into a thin line and tried valiantly to take a grip on her emotions, not the least of which was an embarrassing sense of foolishness. It was going to be difficult acting naturally with the man, worrying all the time over what her mother might say.

She sighed. It was going to be a long and uncomfortable evening...

CHAPTER TWO

HARRIET turned from shutting the front door to find Brad Barrington not smiling but frowning at her. 'I presume you have a sister?' he asked.

She blinked her surprise at his question. 'Why?'

'Well, you are not the girl in the photo on Raymond's desk.'

His words brought full enlightenment. Amanda ... He had wanted to meet Amanda ...

Harriet felt as if someone had punched her in the stomach. 'You must mean Amanda,' she said in what she hoped was a normal voice. But she must have betrayed something for he gave her a sharp look.

She drummed up a smile, but weights seemed to be dragging at the corners of her mouth. 'She's my younger sister. Lovely looking, isn't she?' Harriet managed to keep the smile in place by concentrating on a spot over his shoulder. She couldn't bear to witness the disappointment on his face as she added, 'Sorry, but she's in America at the moment.'

But he merely said, 'Oh? On holiday?'

'No. Living with her lover,' she finished with a flash of vengeance. She was not her sister's keeper and Amanda's reputation had long been shot around Valley's End.

22

If she had expected her visitor to be shocked, she was wrong. 'Lucky man,' he smiled agreeably.

Suddenly, Harriet was looking forward to her mother's reaction to their visitor's shoddiness. She wanted this man disapproved of thoroughly, so that she would never have to endure his company again.

She led him swiftly down the hallway and through the open double doors down into the living-room. 'Mother? Father? Mr Barrington's here.'

Her parents looked up, their faces astonishingly unchanged at sighting their guest's unkempt appearance.

'Brad!' her father boomed, striding up to shake his guest's hand. 'Wonderful to see you again. The beard's coming along, I see. I was just telling Julia about it. Julia...'

He turned to stretch an expansive hand out to his wife. She beamed and moved forward, the three of them launching into small talk. Within seconds her mother was insisting that her guest call her Julia.

Harriet hung back, feeling totally deflated. She had wanted her mother to be shocked, disgusted! To lift up her nose and judge as only she could when confronted with bad social manners. Instead she was smiling at the man and hanging on his every word.

Harriet felt miserable. Miserable and unhappy and alone.

'Sorry about my clothes, Julia,' Barrington was saying smoothly, a Martini in his hand. 'I was unpacking and completely lost track of time. Next thing I knew, it was dark and I couldn't find my watch. I had no idea how long it would take me to get here. I thought it best to arrive, no matter how messy, rather than be abysmally late.' He chuckled. 'Of course I was on your doorstep in no time. I'm used to city traffic, I suppose. These deserted country roads are like something out of another world.'

'Don't you have a clock? Or a radio?'

The trio swung to face Harriet, their expressions showing that all of them had forgotten she was in the room till she spoke.

Mr Barrington's intelligent blue eyes seemed to pick up something. Maybe her tone had held a hint of her wretchedness, or perhaps it was the way she was standing, shoulders tense, arms folded. For he walked over to her, smiling. 'I haven't had time to unpack several of my crates,' he explained. 'No doubt I'll come across the odd clock or radio in there eventually. Not that I need to know the time often. Mostly I just guess.'

'Isn't that a little risky?' Harriet's tone had an edge to it she couldn't seem to control. She had the awful feeling that their guest had sensed her mood, and was trying to smooth her ruffled feathers. It especially annoyed her that he was the only one in the room who even *knew* she had ruffled feathers! 'You might miss the Sunday service,' she finished archly.

He stared at her for just a second, his left eyebrow lifting. She returned his stare without blinking. Be damned with you, Brad Barrington. You and all the rest of the men in this rotten, unfair world!

A ghost of a smile tugged at the corner of his mouth before he turned to face his host and hostess, but not before she saw the spark of amusement in his eyes.

Harriet was taken aback by his response. She had expected a man of his intelligence and undeniable wit to spot her sarcasm. What she hadn't expected was that he would be *amused* by it.

'Did Raymond tell you that Harriet was a writer too?' Julia piped up.

'Oh, no,' Harriet muttered under her breath. 'Mo-ther!' she reproved more loudly.

'A writer?' He turned to look at her, his expression curious now.

'No, I'm not...not really,' she denied with a degree of consternation. 'I'm an English teacher who dabbles in short stories, that's all. I've never been published, except for once or twice in a local paper.'

'But what about the play you've been working on, darling?' Julia insisted. 'She won't let us read it, Brad, but I'm sure she would love for you——'

'Mother, *please*!' Harriet cut in imploringly. 'I'm equally sure Mr Barrington doesn't want to be bothered with my silly scribblings.'

'But you're so wrong,' he said with surprising intensity, and the warmest of smiles. 'I would love to read your play. And it's Brad, not Mr Barrington.'

Harriet looked up into his eyes, searching for the mockery. When she found none an odd heat claimed her cheeks, totally throwing her. She hadn't blushed since she was a teenager, yet here she was, reddening in front of this man like a gauche adolescent. It piqued her considerably, for if there was one thing she was proud of it was her composure. Rarely was she rattled by men these days, especially the ones who oozed false charm.

Yet Brad Barrington's words had reeked of sincerity. And to be honest she could think of no reason why he should say he would like to read it if he did not. Even when watching him on television Harriet had come to the conclusion that here was a man who would always say exactly what he thought. Within reason. He might invent a polite excuse to get out of reading her play, but he would never be coerced against his will.

Grudgingly Harriet liked that trait in him. Liked it a lot.

'You don't have to, you know,' she said, her voice betraying a lingering doubt at his motives.

'I know,' came his smiling yet firm reply. 'I *want* to.'

It was ridiculous, the way his 'I want to' made her feel. It rolled through her heart like a huge wave of delight, melting the icicles of pain, lifting her spirits, soothing her ego. It was as if a light had snapped on in her soul, bringing colour to her face, happiness to her eyes.

'That's very kind of you,' she murmured, looking away before he could see her reaction. Underneath, she knew it was an over-response to an unexpected consideration, and she wondered briefly if he too had ever suffered writer's insecurity, the feeling that no one would ever appreciate what one had written, could ever understand the emotions behind the words.

The penny dropped. Of course he had! What writer hadn't? Only a fellow writer could understand her unwillingness to open herself up to rejection by people who were either uncaring or ignorant. That was why he had offered his expertise, his experience. It was a pity, Harriet thought, that she didn't have the courage to actually let him read her play.

Still, it *was* kind of him.

Her eyes slid back to meet his, only to find them still looking at her with undisguised interest. Her heart gave a decided lurch. Dear heaven, but this man was dynamite!

'Enough of writing talk,' Raymond interrupted. 'Come, Brad, let me top up your drink and you can tell us what plans you have for Mist Mountain...'

The evening went far better than Harriet could have envisaged, with her father gushing forth proudly, her mother preening, and their guest enchanting all three of them with amusing anecdotes of life in the big bad city, as well as tales from his many and varied travels. Where hadn't the man been? Harriet thought breathlessly as she handed around the after-dinner mints.

'I'd love to go to China,' she mused aloud after he'd finished telling them about his latest jaunt around that country. 'I saw that film, *The Last Emperor*, recently, and I couldn't get over the sheer splendour of those magnificent old palaces. To see them first-hand would be...' She shrugged helplessly, unable to find the right word.

'Breathtaking?' Brad suggested. 'Unfortunately, you wouldn't be able to see most of those places on a tourist visa,' he added. 'I gather the producer had special permission to use those settings for the film, but ordinarily they're off-limits.' He picked up his coffee-cup and sipped with slow, savouring swallows, obviously enjoying the flavour of the superb coffee Harriet's mother always brewed.

'Travel is so expensive these days,' Julia sighed.

'Being a writer does have its advantages where that is concerned,' their guest told them as he put down his coffee-cup and leant back in his chair, his mobile face totally at ease as he talked.

How I envy him his supreme confidence, Harriet thought. He would never feel inferior no matter what the company or occasion. There he is, with a three-day growth on his chin and dressed in old clothes, yet he acts like a king, with us his willing subjects, paying homage at his feet.

'Most of it is tax deductible,' he was saying, 'provided you use the places you visit in some way in a book, and that book is published.' He laughed, and Harriet found herself leaning forwards, her chin supported in her hands, unable to take her eyes off him. 'Of course it was hard finding some way of working my trip to China into my last book,' he said breezily, 'since it was entirely set on the Gold Coast in Queensland. But my tax accountant insisted so I gave my hero a murky past that included a couple of lost years behind the bamboo curtain. Those vital chapters saved me donating a few extra thousand to our dear treasurer.'

'Oh, how clever of you!' Julia exclaimed.

'Pays to have a smart accountant!' Raymond said smugly.

Harriet frowned. Despite her admiration of their guest it went against her grain that a plot could be manipulated for tax reasons, a character made to do something simply because it would save its creator money. It was somehow...amoral?

Amoral... An interesting word, that, she pondered. It wasn't the same as immoral. It didn't mean evil, or deliberately bad. It meant without conscience, with no sense of right or wrong. An *immoral* man might seduce a woman for the wicked thrill of taking her virtue. An *amoral* man would seduce a woman simply because he enjoyed the physical pleasure, not even being aware of any emotional damage he might wreak.

Stomach suddenly aflutter, Harriet glanced over at their visitor, her eyes coming to rest on his mouth. It was nothing special. Perhaps a little wide, with the lower lip disproportionately full. But it smiled readily, with a habit of lifting in one corner, a mouth full of life and laughter.

And seduction...

Even as she watched it, the lips were pulling back, that corner lifting, and as her eyes jolted up to meet his she realised he was smiling at *her* with his provocative smile.

She should have looked away, should have protected herself from the sexual potency of this man, but she couldn't. And didn't. Instead, she kept staring at him, enjoying the play of the lines on his face, the way that light twinkled boldly in his eyes whenever he looked at a woman. *Any* woman... She was not so much of a fool that she thought he was exercising his charm exclusively for her. But it was devastating, nevertheless.

'Have you read my latest effort, Harriet?' he asked. 'Or aren't my books to your taste?'

'Harriet reads simply *everything*,' her mother inserted before she could answer.

'Not everything, Mother,' she retorted, a fraction sharply. But it was herself she was annoyed with. Hadn't life taught her *anything*? 'I've read your first two,' she admitted with more care, 'and enjoyed them very much, but I haven't got round to... I'm sorry, the name of your latest release has slipped my mind. What is it? I'll pick a copy up as soon as I see one.'

'It's called *High-Rise*. But for heaven's sake don't go buying the thing, especially not in hardcover. It's outrageously expensive. I'll give you one of my presentation copies. I have several packed away in a crate doing nothing but collecting dust. No! Don't object. I won't take no for an answer.'

Harriet shook her head in a type of ironic bemusement. 'That's very generous of you,' she murmured, thinking privately that Brad Barrington would rarely get no for an answer, anyway. Particularly in certain matters...

Her train of thought had her colouring again. And hating herself for it. She hadn't been this stirred up by a man since Graham. It was disconcerting because it was so darned futile!

Raymond scraped back his chair and stood up. 'Care for a port, Brad? I have a nice bottle here you might like.'

'Love it,' Brad beamed, and Harriet acknowledged what a perfect guest he was. Ironic, considering her first impression of him on the porch. Somehow his crumpled clothes and stubbly chin had faded into insignificance beneath the onslaught of his vivid personality. It crossed her mind that Amanda would have been bowled over by him. And he by her, no doubt.

Thank God her sister was in America. It was going to be hard enough, having to endure this man ignoring her after tonight. But it would have been unbearable to watch him pursue Amanda. Harriet could imagine exactly how it would have been. The repeated phone calls... the nightly rendezvous... Amanda's empty bed in the mornings...

'Aren't you having a port, Harriet?' Brad asked, when her father sat down without pouring her one.

She blinked, her mind having been torn back to the present with an accompanying flush of embarrassment. It wasn't like her to be so melodramatic, to let her mind run away with herself. 'No, I...' She stopped, an unexpected rebellious surge making her change her mind from protecting her father's thoughtlessness. 'Actually, I wouldn't mind one,' she finished brusquely.

Brad was on his feet in an instant. 'Don't get up, Raymond,' he insisted. 'I'm nearest.' He swept the bottle up and was down the table in a flash, dextrously pouring Harriet a healthy swig into her empty wine glass. 'Can't have a fellow writer dying of thirst, can we?' he chuckled, rewarding her with another of his heart-lurching smiles.

Her hand shook as she lifted the drink to her lips, so much so that she had to curl her other hand around her trembling fingers to stop the port from spilling. Thankfully, Brad was already in retreat so he didn't notice.

But her mother did... Her mother with the smug smile on her face.

Harriet groaned inwardly. Didn't her mother know what type of man they were dealing with? He did this sort of thing on automatic pilot. Any flirtatious gesture on his part did not mean that he found her especially desirable. He would act the same way with an eighty-two-year-old great-grandmother.

In a way, Harriet was relieved as the evening drew to an end. When dear Mr Barrington never rang or called back, her mother would have to give up her silly matchmaking ideas. Julia Weatherspoon was an old-fashioned woman and would never countenance chasing after a man. In her world men were the hunters, women the prey.

Perhaps that's part of my problem, Harriet thought with sudden insight. Underneath it all, I take after my mother, always expecting and waiting for a man to make the first move. Crazy really. These days it's just as common for a woman to ring up and ask a man out. Hadn't she heard of women's liberation? Yet somehow...

She frowned and slid a sideways glance over at their guest. Amanda wouldn't let this man get away so easily, came the irritating thought.

They had moved to have another glass of port on the chesterfield lounge suite that faced the terrace overlooking the valley. In summer they might have gone outside on to the terrace, but August was not only cold but windy. So they admired the moonlit valley from behind the safety and warmth of the plate glass windows, a fire burning slowly in the combustion stove nestling in the corner.

'I'd like to do something similar to this in my place,' Brad said. 'Rip out the wall on the side that overlooks the valley and put in glass.' It wasn't the first time that evening he had mentioned the changes he wanted to make to the old homestead he'd bought on Mist Mountain.

'Are you going to do the renovations yourself?' Julia asked, wide-eyed.

'Heck, no! I'd be the worst handyman in the world. Raymond here has recommended a couple of local men who are good at that sort of thing but I won't be doing anything for at least six months. By then I'll have the rough draft of my next novel finished and I'll need a break. Meanwhile, I couldn't stand the noise of workmen. My concentration would suffer.'

'But I thought you liked a lot of noise when you worked?' Harriet put in without thinking.

He turned surprised eyes to where she was sitting on the other end of the four-seater leather sofa. Her mother and father were occupying the armchairs situated adjacent to them.

'Where on earth did you get that idea?' he asked.

She was taken aback. 'You said so yourself...on the *Tonight* show on television...'

His look was faintly sardonic. 'Dear, sweet Harriet ... If I told my public the truth, that I practically locked myself in a dark cupboard when I wrote, without seeing the light of day for weeks, they wouldn't like it at all. They want to hear what a wild boy I am, that I actually *do* the sort of things my heroes do.'

'And *don't* you?' she quizzed with her heart in her mouth.

He flashed a blatantly knowing look at her, and her toes curled up in her shoes. 'Sometimes, perhaps,' he confessed. 'But certainly not while I'm writing. I give the whole of myself when I write. I have neither the time nor the energy to do anything else. And I mean *anything*!' he finished, his wickedly dancing eyes telling her exactly what he meant by anything.

Harriet tore her own eyes away, landing them on her mother who was looking just a trifle perplexed. Her father, however, had sunk into the depths of his armchair, dragging away on a cigar. Whenever Raymond Weatherspoon was not in on a conversation he clicked off.

'I must read one of your books, Brad,' Julia said slowly, her expression vaguely troubled.

Do that, Mother, Harriet thought with meaning. Then I won't have to hear another word about how suitable dear Mr Barrington is as a husband, since a less suitable candidate for marriage I have yet to see! A woman would not be able to trust him out of her sight for a moment!

She nearly spilt her port when he unexpectedly leant over and touched her wrist. 'And when are you going to let me read this play of yours, Harriet?'

Her face must have betrayed her near panic, for he added gently, 'I'm a kind critic, I swear.'

'Well, I...I...'

'Why don't you bring it over to my place tomorrow, and then I can give you a copy of my new book to bring back? I might even inveigle you into helping me arrange my books in my bookcases. A woman's touch is always invaluable in matters of house and hearth, don't you think, Julia?'

Any momentary worry disappeared from her mother's face as Brad bestowed his bewitching smile upon her. 'I couldn't agree more,' she beamed back. 'And Harriet is the most splendid little organiser. Never a thing out of place in her room. Not like her sister, who drops things all over...' She broke off when she saw Harriet stiffen.

Julia glanced back to the handsome man sitting next to her daughter and the thought struck—thank the lord Amanda's in America!

Brad heaved a contented-sounding sigh, placed his empty glass down on the side-table and stood up. 'It's been a most enjoyable evening, Julia...Raymond...but it's time I was going.'

They all got to their feet and somehow Harriet found herself given the job of escorting their guest to the front door. And as she walked with him she remembered that the matter of her coming over the next day had hardly been settled.

She wanted to go. There was no point in denying it. But his motive in inviting her was vaguely troubling. She had heard of men who weren't discriminating over what women they tried to seduce, but she had never met one—before.

Harriet flicked a sneaky glance over her shoulder at him as she stopped to open the door. Heavens, but on his feet he was a big man, with big broad shoulders and a massive chest and . . .

'Well, Harriet? When can I expect you tomorrow?'

She had to look at him properly now, actually meet his eyes. They held nothing but polite enquiry and Harriet realised his invitation was no more than a friendly gesture. A kindness, inspired perhaps by pity. He had seen the way her father ignored her. She was sure he had.

It was perverse of her to feel disappointment at the realisation. But disappointed she was.

She turned away and ushered him out on to the porch before answering. 'Are you sure you really want me to come over tomorrow?' she asked point-blank.

'But of course!' he insisted. 'Whyever not?'

'It's just that . . .'

'Oh, I see,' he said immediately, his face frowning deeply for the first time that night. 'I didn't think of that. Stupid of me.'

She was puzzled. 'Think of what?'

'That your boyfriend wouldn't like it. There has to be one, a girl like you . . .'

He couldn't have said anything more pleasurable to Harriet's ears. She fairly blossomed with his indirect compliment, so much so that he looked quite startled when she turned her smiling face up to him. 'As a matter of fact, I don't have a steady boyfriend... at the moment,' she added, having to work at keeping her delight under control.

His arched eyebrows arched some more. 'I have to admit that surprises me.'

He sounded so sincere. Harriet warmed to him even more, if that were possible.

'So what's the problem?' he asked, then grinned. 'Surely Sunday service doesn't take up all your day!'

Her laughter was light and happy. 'I do go to church but quite early. No... I didn't want to impose, that's all. I'm sure aspiring writers are always pestering you with stuff to read. Not only that—I don't seriously think my play will ever be published or performed. It's a private and personal thing, you see. A hobby, really.'

His look carried reproach. 'You don't believe that, Harriet Weatherspoon, any more than I do. What's the point of slaving away over the right words if no one ever reads them? Come, now... I can see you're a refreshingly straightforward girl. Intelligent too. My bet is that your play is good. Bloody good! So don't belittle it or yourself. Have confidence!'

She blinked her bewilderment. The last thing she had expected from their perfect guest had been a lecture. 'It's all very well for you to say that,' she returned with feeling. 'You're a success!'

'That wasn't always the case,' came his rueful reply. 'Now, I don't want to hear any more of this rubbish. I'll expect you at my place around eleven, and bring that manuscript with you or I'll drive you back and collect it myself. OK?'

'OK,' she repeated in a dazed voice.

'Good.' He turned away and walked briskly down the steps over to where a sleek black Porsche lay half hidden in the shadows. 'And tell your mother you won't be home till late,' he threw back at her as he wrenched open the door and slid behind the wheel.

She was still standing there with her mouth open when the Porsche growled to life and sprang up the lane.

CHAPTER THREE

HARRIET was relieved to get away from the house the following morning. Her mother had simply not stopped raving over Mr Barrington for a second, except for the hour they were actually in church. In the car on the way there and back, then over breakfast, the compliments had flowed non-stop: wasn't he handsome, charming, witty, widely travelled, et cetera et cetera et cetera?

It irritated Harriet considerably. OK, so he was all of those things. But he wasn't perfect! Far from it, she suspected. Neither did she believe that he was at all taken by her, as her mother kept implying.

Having woken this morning with a clear head and mind, Harriet had again seen Brad's invitation for what it was—a friendly overture by a friendly man. Nothing more.

Harriet had observed over the years what happened when a male was really attracted to a female. The smitten individuals couldn't keep their eyes off the objects of their desire. They angled to be closer physically, finding any excuse for contact. They telephoned almost as soon as they had left and were back on the doorstep within no time, bringing never-ending presents and bending over backwards in their efforts to please.

Amanda's boyfriends had provided her with many examples of male courting.

No... Harriet was positive Brad wanted no more from her than he had spelt out. Some help with his unpacking, in exchange for which she would get a free copy of his book as well as an opinion on her play. Perhaps he intended to sit down and read it straight away, since he expected her to stay all day. Or perhaps he had more unpacking than the usual bachelor.

Either way she was sure his invitation held no ulterior motives. Any man who had just had a stunning beauty like Lydia Richmond in his bed was not going to replace her with Harriet Weatherspoon!

Harriet laughed aloud at the ridiculous idea as she reversed her red Holden Astra out of the garage. She turned the wheel to face the vehicle down the narrow lane, a check of her watch revealing that she had more than enough time to reach Brad's place before eleven.

Five minutes later she had passed through the small township and was approaching the mountain turn-off when she spotted something out of the corner of her eye. It was old Mrs Gallagher, out in her front garden, waving to her as she drove past. Harriet was pleased to see her neighbour looking so well, thereby depriving that rotten nephew of hers from his ill-deserved inheritance for at least a while yet.

She wound down her window and waved back. But she quickly wound it up again as a sharp wind entered the car and ruffled her hair.

Spring could not come soon enough, she thought as she slowed down at the next intersection. It would be a pleasant change to have a sun that contained some warmth, and breezes that were not so bitter.

But she quickly put aside thoughts of the weather, concentrating instead on the road that wound its precarious way up Mist Mountain. It was worse than she remembered, a disgrace really, nothing more than a narrow strip of rough-edged tar slapped down over the old bullock paths of bygone days. On one side sheer rock-face rose up into massive trees. On the other, it dropped precipitously down, less than a metre from the edge, the dense treetops and undergrowth disguising the danger. The only compensation was that Harriet was unlikely to meet a vehicle coming the other way, since it was a dead-end road that only serviced a few properties.

Nevertheless, she was quite relieved to reach the plateau at the top of the ridgeway and turn off on to the private road that led to Brad's property. There was no gate to mark the driveway, and anyone not familiar with the area would have gone straight past it. But Harriet knew the place quite well, this particular farm having once been owned by parents of a girl she had gone to school with.

When her friend's family had moved away, a queer religious sect had bought it, setting themselves up as a commune. There had been tales of weird rites and sex orgies—perhaps more speculation than truth—but the conservative community had not been upset when the sect's leader was arrested for growing marijuana and the place subsequently put up for sale.

But hadn't it been let run wild? Harriet's eyes swept around the once clear undulating hills with dismay. There was scrub everywhere and what fences there were were falling down. Still, she supposed it would hardly worry Brad if he had to spend a bit of money on it. He had plenty.

The road swung around a corner and up a sharp rise, at the crest of which the house came into view, perched on a further knoll a hundred yards ahead. It was a typical Australian farmhouse, a large rectangular wooden building with a high pitched roof, deep narrow windows and wide verandas all around. Even if Harriet had never been inside she would have known that it was bisected from front to back by a hallway which served as a most efficient breezeway to cool the interior. Doors would open from this central hallway to rooms on either side, bedrooms first then living areas, with a large homy kitchen across the back. The floor plans of most of these homesteads were basically the same.

He was waiting for her on the veranda, sitting in an old rocking-chair, looking as though he had been there since time began. The roughly growing beard, the faded jeans, the old checked shirt, gave him a mountain-man image which his formidably large body only added to. He looked like a lumberjack, not a writer.

He didn't get up as she braked to a halt in front of the house, this lack of enthusiasm at her arrival bringing a sigh to her lips.

'So much for his being smitten, Mother,' she muttered under her breath.

Yet oddly enough it was almost reassuring to have her conclusions about Brad confirmed. She would hate him to make a play for her out of a temporary loneliness, or sheer boredom. That would mean he really was like those male characters in his books, the ones who used women merely as playthings or diversions, without a shred of caring for them. Not that he had a chance of seducing *her* that easily anyway. The depressing lack of opportunity so far in her life had not swayed Harriet from the firm belief that she wanted to be *loved* before being made love to.

He nodded and waved down to her as she alighted, but remained where he was, still rocking. She leant back into the car to pick up her manuscript from the passenger seat, aware she was presenting a splendid view of her trim backside. But she didn't imagine for one moment that the sight of her bejeaned bottom would send this hero's pulse racing. She knew exactly the sort of bottom he went for. It had been described in meticulous detail in his books. And it was far from boyish...

Harriet straightened, hugging the bulky folder against her pale blue jumper, suddenly conscious that her heart was thudding inside her chest. Foolish, she realised, to have begun thinking about his books. They were so sexual that they invariably put one's mind on that track. It was to her credit that she managed to look up at the creator of those unforgettably erotic scenes with nothing more than a friendly smile.

'You look as if you've found an old friend in that chair,' she called out from where she was standing.

His smile dazzled back at her and her heart turned over. Hell... So much for all her holier-

than-thou beliefs! Harriet suspected with an under-
mining burst of honesty that if this man ever wanted
to he could have her in bed within no time.

She grew hotly aware of his eyes upon her as she
moved towards the steps. All at once her jeans felt
uncomfortably tight against her thighs, and she just
knew that her cheeks were once again carrying an
uncharacteristic blush. Annoyed, she deliberately
put more purpose into her strides, lifting her chin
and tossing back her hair in defiance of her own
silly self.

His smile widened to a grin as she fairly bounded
on to the veranda and he made a show of pointing
at his watch. 'Two minutes late,' he announced.
'I'm afraid I will have to keep you back after school
as a punishment.'

She had to laugh, the thought mocking her that
to be kept back by him was hardly a punishment.
But he knew that, didn't he, the devil?

'Couldn't I just write a hundred times that I will
not be late again, sir?' she parried, but keeping her
expression light and cool.

He pretended to consider her suggestion.
'Perhaps I will let you off entirely if you are on
your best behaviour for the rest of the day. But you
must promise to obey my every command.'

'Yes, sir. Of course, sir!'

He rose then, the sudden upwards action leaving
the chair rocking wildly. Like my pulse-rate, Harriet
admitted, her eyes drawn to the long muscular legs
striding towards her. Steady on, now, girl, a voice
warned her. Don't make a fool of yourself!

'Is this the masterpiece?' he was saying with hand outstretched.

She swallowed, having temporarily forgotten her play. 'I . . .' She held it out hesitatingly.

He took the folder, glancing first at its thickness before slanting a thoughtful look down at her. 'Nervous about my reading it?'

'Of course,' she admitted with a covering laugh.

Those deeply set eyes unnerved her with their intuitive intelligence.

'Why?' he demanded. 'Because you think it's no good or because it's autobiographical?'

She blinked her surprise, her lips parting. The story was not strictly her own life but there certainly were parallels, and all of her heroine's thoughts and feelings had at some stage been her own. It was the main reason she would never let her mother or father read it.

'You don't have to answer that,' he said, an understanding smile warming his eyes. 'Your face has done it for you. But don't worry, your secrets are safe with me. I don't have a judgemental bone in my body. Neither am I a gossipmonger. My dear Harriet, you could be a high-class call girl and I wouldn't turn a hair or breathe a word.'

'That's a relief,' she countered drily.

His expression registered true shock. 'My God, you *aren't*, are you?'

It tickled her fancy that he could even think such a thing. 'You'll have to read the play and find out, won't you?' she tossed off in a cavalier fashion, but chuckling inside. 'Now, where are all these books

I'm supposed to be helping you unpack?' she said, turning away before a smile broke out.

She walked over to the doorway where she stopped and glanced over her shoulder, barely restraining her laughter when she saw his face, comically transfixed with shock. She couldn't resist saying, 'Come along, Mr Barrington, you might have all day but I don't. I have a special client to see this evening.'

'Client?' he repeated, wide blue eyes blinking.

It was hard to imagine anyone being shocked by the remedial reading lesson that she gave every Sunday evening to a lad with dyslexia, but Harriet said quite truthfully, 'Yes... A young man I see every week. He came to me a couple of months ago with this rather delicate problem. He was quite shy and embarrassed about it. But I assured him that with patience, and the right guidance...'

She couldn't keep it up. She burst out laughing.

'Who would have thought that the highly sensible young woman I met last night would be a tease?' Brad reprimanded, a wry grin curving back his attractive mouth.

'I wasn't lying,' she laughed. 'I do have a pupil coming tonight for a lesson. A reading lesson. He has dyslexia.'

'Hmm. Are you sure that's all he's coming for? How old is this pupil?'

'Eighteen.'

'Some boys are men at eighteen,' he said pointedly. 'Watch yourself.'

She looked up at Brad in amazement. He'd sounded jealous. How positively astounding!

But then he grinned, and she realised he was teasing her back in return.

'Enough of this nonsense,' he announced. 'Down the hall and the third door on the right. March!'

She marched, laughing all the way, thinking to herself that even if Brad Barrington was a scoundrel, he was still the most charming, most amusing man she had met in ages.

Almost two hours and ten crates of books later her only feeling was weariness. 'How many books do you own?' she sighed, slotting another huge dictionary on the shelf she had reserved for textbooks.

Brad finished ripping the tape off the next cardboard crate before looking up and shrugging. 'Too many, obviously. I was going to take some down to a second-hand book store before the move but I couldn't decide which ones to part with. In the end I just ordered another bookcase and brought them all.'

Harriet glanced around the room, which would have been reasonably spacious if it weren't for all the bookcases. There were nine of various sizes, three large ones along the one unencumbered wall, a smaller one on either side of the glass doors that led out on to the veranda, more flanking the fireplace and the doorway. This left barely enough room for the furniture, which Brad had arranged facing the fireplace in semicircular fashion. There were three large old armchairs with padded armrests, two standing lamps, two small tables and a fluffy white rug. They made a comfy reading-room,

but were hardly sufficient seating for entertaining
on any scale.

Clearly Brad had no intention of doing so since
this room was supposed to be the lounge-room. And
the dining-room, she had noted, had already been
converted into his study, full of desks, filing cabi-
nets and computer equipment.

'I'll eat in the kitchen,' he told her when she
pointed this out. 'If I get desperate for a dining-
room I'll convert one of the bedrooms.'

Harriet recalled that there were four bedrooms,
but they were located at the front of the house, two
on either side of the hallway as you came in the
front door. The one and only bathroom sat between
the two smaller bedrooms, its antiquated facilities
a testimony to a time better forgotten, Harriet
thought. But she kept this opinion to herself, remembering what her mother had said about her
having too frank a tongue.

'Here are the copies of my new book,' Brad said,
extracting one from the crate he'd just opened and
handing it over to her.

She gazed down at the cover, which was eye-
catching with a near-naked girl stretched out on the
golden sand, the horizon of skyscrapers behind her
at odds with the breathtaking beauty of the beach.
One could hardly take offence at a spot of semi-
nudity these days, Harriet realised, but she found
the expression on the voluptuous blonde's face dis-
tastefully explicit. The half-closed eyes, the parted
lips...

A sigh had escaped before she could bite it back.

'Too much?'

She glanced up to see Brad looking at her with a rueful expression in his usually smiling eyes. Surely he wasn't *embarrassed* by the picture, was he?

'No, no,' she said, but not convincingly.

'Come, now, Harriet. Be honest. You think it's tacky, don't you?'

'Well, I ... Well ... Yes, just a bit.'

His own sigh showed irritation. 'It wasn't what I wanted,' he growled, reaching down into the box to drag some more books out with an angry jerk, 'but you know publishers.'

'No,' she said. 'I don't, actually.'

His chin jerked up to glare at her, and then he laughed. 'You really are a one, Harriet, do you know that? You say what you think. Such refreshing honesty is rare.'

Harriet looked down, perturbed that the slightest compliment from this man could affect her with such intensity. 'Some people don't find that a particularly pleasant trait in me,' she muttered, busying herself with some more books.

'To hell with them. I do! If there's one thing I can't stand it's hypocrisy and mealy-mouthed people.'

'Me, too,' she said with meaning, and blew some dust off the covers.

When he didn't say anything back, she finally glanced up, and was surprised to see him staring at her with the oddest look on his face. It was a second before she registered that it might be pain.

'Brad?' she asked. 'Are you all right?' She took a tentative step towards him. 'Brad? What's wrong?'

He blinked, then dragged in a deep breath. He tried to smile, the corners of his mouth twitching, before giving up the effort. 'It's all right,' he said, recovering sufficiently to smile, but she could see it was an effort. 'A spasm in my chest. It . . . it took me by surprise.'

'Do you have a problem with your heart?' she asked anxiously.

Again that flicker of something, even though he was still smiling. 'At my age?' he joked. 'More likely indigestion, which reminds me it's time for all hard-working unpackers to have lunch. What would you like? Soup? Pies? Toasted sandwiches? Basic menu, I'm afraid.'

'Soup and toast sound good,' she murmured distractedly.

'My thoughts exactly. Come on... Follow me...'

She stood there, watching him leave the room, still puzzled over what had happened. Could a serious health problem be his reason for exiling himself to the country? It was possible, she supposed. But then she shook her head, telling herself that she was being melodramatic again. Never had she encountered a more healthy looking specimen of virile manhood.

No, she decided as she traipsed out to the kitchen. It had to have been indigestion, as he said.

But when she saw his face again, still darkly frowning, she wasn't so sure.

CHAPTER FOUR

HARRIET first heard the noise as she was taking her last swallow of chicken soup. It was a tiny, high-pitched sound, seemingly coming from underneath the table.

She bent down, stared at the empty vinyl floor, then straightened. 'Did you hear that?' she asked Brad, who'd been unnaturally quiet during lunch.

'Hear what?'

She frowned. 'I don't know exactly. It sounded like a mouse, I think.'

'Could be,' he admitted. 'I've had to put down a few mousetraps in the pantry.'

She glanced over towards the small store-room that adjoined the kitchen but knew the noise hadn't come from there. Perhaps the mouse had scuttled under the refrigerator, or the stove. She shrugged. Being a country girl, mice held no fears for her.

But then the noise came again, and this time Brad heard it as well. One, then another pitiful little cry.

'Kittens!' they both said in unison.

'Under the house?' Harriet suggested.

'Oh, hell,' Brad groaned. 'They probably belong to the poor old cat I ran over last night. It charged out under the front wheels as I came up to the house. I buried it in the bush but it didn't occur to me that there might have been kittens.'

51

'They must be getting hungry,' Harriet murmured, her heart turning over. 'Poor little mites...'

Brad sighed. 'And I suppose you want me to crawl under the house and find them?'

'Would you?' she asked hopefully.

He pulled a face which showed reluctance and resignation. 'Off to the rescue,' he said, scraping back his chair and getting to his feet.

There were four of them, pitifully starved little bundles of bone and fur. Three black and white, and one all white which was tinier than the others, if that was possible. They carried them inside where Brad found an empty shoebox and an old jumper to line it.

'Do you have an eye-dropper?' Harriet asked. 'They're too young to lap. Their eyes aren't even open yet.'

Brad shook his head. 'Sorry. Can't we take them to the RSPCA?'

'There isn't any animal welfare shelter around here,' Harriet informed him, 'and the local vet isn't the sort of chap to take in orphan kittens. He's a bit on the hard side and would probably put them down. I suppose I could take them home, but Mum hates cats ... She won't tolerate them in the house. Says they scratch the furniture.'

'Which they do,' Brad put in pointedly.

'Not you too,' Harriet berated. 'Human beings have a responsibility to look after poor defenceless creatures like these, not turn a blind eye to their suffering. That's cruel!'

'OK, don't get your dander up! Suggest something.'

'We could drive down to the after-hours chemist and buy an eye-dropper and some baby food, I guess. But that's only a temporary measure. Let's face it, these babies will need feeding every few hours and I have to go to school tomorrow...' She looked pleadingly up at Brad, who shook his head vigorously.

'Oh, no, you don't! I'm prepared to help in some way but I'm not getting into that. When I write, I go off into another dimension. It's hours sometimes before I re-enter the real world. By then these "babies" might have expired and I'd have to put up with those big brown eyes of yours looking at me as though I were a mass murderer! No, my dear Harriet, we have to find another solution.'

An inspiration struck. 'I have it! Mrs Gallagher!'

'Mrs Gallagher? Who the devil is Mrs Gallagher?'

'An old lady I know who's as lonely as one can be and who adores cats. She'd be a perfect baby-sitter till we can find homes for these precious darlings.' Harriet picked up the little white one, who was extra timid, and held it against her cheek, crooning softly to it. 'We'll have to find an extra special home for you, won't we, sweetie?'

Brad pulled another wry face. 'Off we go, then. I trust this saintly Mrs Gallagher will be home?'

'Oh, yes, I saw her this morning on my way up here.'

'We'll take my car,' he suggested. 'You direct.'

Mrs Gallagher was not only home but delighted to have both the kittens and the visitors.

'And you have an eye-dropper?' Harriet reiterated as they were led into the front parlour. Impossible to call the room anything else, she thought, with its lace doilies and upright brocade chairs.

'Better than that,' the old lady said, leaving them briefly to return with a tiny bottle and teat that looked as if it had been designed for a doll.

Which it had, they learned.

'I've raised orphan kittens before,' she informed them proudly. 'Of course it was some years ago but I don't think I've lost the knack.' A happy smile lit up the wrinkled but still handsome face. 'You and your young man needn't worry, Harriet.'

'Oh, he's not my...' Harriet broke off, embarrassed.

Mrs Gallagher turned a curious face to Brad.

'I'm just a friend,' he told her. 'Harriet's family have been making me feel welcome since I moved to Valley's End a couple of days ago. I bought the old farm up on Mist Mountain.'

'Aah... The author fellow.'

Brad showed his surprise and Harriet laughed. 'You don't honestly expect to keep anything secret around here, do you?'

He lifted his eyebrows then shook his head. 'Not any more I won't.'

The kittens began mewing in the box. 'I'd ask you to stay for a cup of tea,' Mrs Gallagher said, 'but as you can see I'd better get on with feeding the hungry hordes. Now, don't forget to drop by to see how they're getting on in a few days,' she added as she shepherded them to the front door.

'You *are* going to take one, aren't you, young man? You'll need company up on that lonely mountain of yours.'

'Well, I...'

'He wants the white one,' Harriet piped up, holding her breath and waiting for him to deny it.

But he didn't. He merely smiled at her with a sort of rueful resignation. 'The white one,' he repeated, nodding almost wearily.

Brad was so silent on the drive back up the mountain that Harriet began to feel guilty, so much so that, by the time he turned the Porsche from the dangerous road on to the relatively safe dirt track, she could keep quiet no longer. 'I'm sorry if I put you on the spot,' she burst out. 'I know I shouldn't have.'

He darted her a sideways glance, meeting her worried eyes with a reassuring smile. 'Fat lot of good that does me now,' he reproached, but not unkindly. 'Who's cat is it going to be, anyway? Mine? Or yours by proxy?'

'Oh, definitely yours!'

'That's good, because I'm going to call it Brigit.'

'How do you know it's a girl cat?'

He slid a sardonic smirk her way. 'Trust me. It'll be a girl.'

'OK, but why Brigit?'

'When you've read *High-Rise*, you'll know,' was his cryptic answer.

Harriet frowned, the mention of her reading his book reminding her that he would soon be reading her play. Suddenly, she didn't want him to, didn't want him to see through the fiction to the fact. She had the impression he thought her a confident, well-adjusted person, not the pained, lonely girl who walked through those pages, full of doubts and insecurities. Since she could hardly stop him reading it now she had to say something to stop him jumping to the right conclusions.

'By the way, Brad,' she began as he drew the car to a halt behind hers. 'I want you to know that my play isn't autobiographical, though I did glean a lot of my ideas from life. My heroine, Henrietta, is based on the experiences of a girl I knew at university. I was nervous before because I'm worried you'll think it very amateurish, that's all.'

He switched off the engine and turned to give her a penetrating look. The sudden silence made Harriet realise how close they were in the car. Her eyes became fixed on his mouth, which was within such easy kissing distance of hers.

'Do you want the truth, Harriet?' he said with unexpected brusqueness.

She blinked, glancing up to find his eyes firmly on her face. 'The truth?'

'About your play... Do you want me to tell you the truth after I've read it; whether I think it has any potential or not? Because if you don't then there's not much point in my reading it.' His voice was curt, even aggressive. 'I won't water down my views in deference to your female sensitivity. That would be wasting both your time and mine.'

She swallowed, recalling wryly that she had once admired his frankness. But being on the end of it was not quite as easy to take. 'I want you to be completely honest,' she said aloud, hoping that she meant it. She didn't realise she was frowning at his unexpectedly curt manner.

'Don't worry,' he added, his mouth softening into a soothing smile. 'I won't be cruel. It will be the truth tempered with understanding. A constructive rather than a destructive criticism, fair enough?'

Her smile carried relief. 'Fair enough.'

'Well, Harriet? It's almost four o'clock. I suppose you'll be wanting to get home soon if you've got that chap coming later for his lesson.'

Harriet tried to hide her dismay at being so summarily dismissed. After all, what had she expected? That he would sweep her back inside the house, insist she stay for dinner, beg her to put off her lesson this once? Brad's words to Mrs Gallagher resurfaced from where they'd been lurking unhappily in her mind. 'I'm just a friend... Harriet's family have been making me feel welcome...'

Oh, silly, silly Harriet!

'Yes, I'd better be going,' she said without showing the slightest emotion. Practice makes perfect, she thought with dry satisfaction.

Brad pulled the keys out of his ignition and dropped them into his shirt pocket. 'Thanks for all your help with the books,' he said matter-of-factly.

'No trouble.'

'I'll read your play this week and give you a call, OK?'

'OK.' So that was it, she thought wretchedly. One phone call, then nothing. Oh, well, it was only logical. Considering.

They both fell silent for a few seconds.

'I'll tell you what,' Brad resumed, twisting slightly in his seat to face her more easily. 'If you've nothing else on, how about I take you out for dinner next Friday night? We can discuss your play over the meal. Far better than talking on the phone. I'm inclined to be long-winded when I start yakking about something I've read and my ear aches after half an hour. Well? What do you say?'

She had difficulty controlling her upsurge of spirits, despite the obviously platonic nature of his proposed date. 'I'd like that,' she said carefully.

'If I pick you up around five we could drop in to see the kittens first and then go on to dinner from there. What say we go over to the coast to Coff's Harbour? I stayed at a resort there briefly last year and there are a lot of good restaurants to choose from.'

Harriet didn't mind that suggestion at all. Coff's Harbour was a good hour's drive away, which meant she would have his company much longer than if they went to a local place.

'I'll be looking forward to it,' she confessed, unable this time to suppress a happy smile.

For a split second his handsome face was marred by an oddly troubled look. But just as quickly the twisted features smoothed away. 'No more than I,' he returned blithely.

It crossed her mind again that perhaps he wasn't well, that he was still in some sort of pain or discomfort, that he was getting rid of her because he wanted to be alone. But she quickly reasoned that this was her own stupid imagination again, trying desperately to find some reason why he didn't want her to stay longer.

'I'll pop inside and get the copy of my book,' he offered, opening the car door and climbing out from behind the wheel.

Harriet was in her car and ready to go when he returned. She took the book from his hands through the open window. 'Thanks. I hope you're ready for an honest opinion on Friday night, also,' she added, waving the novel at him.

'Naturally. And speaking of honest opinions...' he went on.

'Yes?'

'Tell me what you think of my beard.'

She blinked up at him, then let her focus rest on the rough stubble. He had the sort of face, of course, that would look good with a full beard. But as her eyes grazed over his chin all she could think of was what it would feel like to have the roughness rasp across her face, her throat...

Her eyes widened as she felt an uncomfortable prickling in her breasts. She cleared her throat, then swallowed. 'Shave it off,' she announced perfunctorily.

He rubbed his rough chin. 'All of it?'

'Definitely. A moustache makes a man look shifty and a beard hides his intelligence.' And what a load of old rubbish, she thought silently.

Brad rubbed his chin. 'Are you saying I look like a sleazy numbskull?'

'Not quite, Brad,' came her dry reply. 'Remember, I saw you on television without a beard and you look better clean-shaven.'

'But I detest shaving!' he protested.

'I detest cleaning my car,' she countered.

His gaze swept over the spotless vehicle. 'Are you telling me you want me to shave before Friday night?' he asked with a grin.

'Not at all. I'm merely saying you look much better without the stubble.'

'And being a friend you tell it as it is, eh?'

'You did ask,' she reminded him.

He shook his head with mild exasperation. 'I have a feeling that knowing you, Harriet, is going to be a trial. In one day I have acquired a cat and am in danger of losing a beard, which is contrary since I like beards, and abhor cats. Are you a bossy-boots with everyone?'

Her shrug was light as she determined not to let her feelings for this man get out of control, or lose perspective. 'I suppose so. Teachers usually are. I'm sorry. Keep the beard, by all means. And I'll find another home for the kitten.'

'Don't you dare! Brigit and I will learn to co-exist. In time. It's better than having you look at me with that disapproving glare of yours.'

She was taken aback. 'When have I ever looked at you like that?'

He leant against the car window, bringing his face disturbingly close. 'You should have seen your face when you answered the door last night. If looks could kill I'd not only be dead but incinerated.'

'Well, you did look like a refugee.'

He rubbed his chin again, and grinned some more. 'I suppose I did. But to your parents' credit they didn't bat an eyelid.'

'My mother is a lady,' she assured him. 'My father, a businessman.'

'Do I detect a certain cynicism in the latter half of that statement?'

'Perhaps... Now, will you get that great lump of a head of yours out of my window and let me go home?'

He straightened, a wicked light dancing in his eyes. 'My, my, you are *so* complimentary! Most women find my head quite attractive.'

She gave him a tart look. 'I'm not most women,' she threw up at him, detesting him suddenly for changing over to the flirtatious charm he had used on her the previous evening. She much preferred the casually friendly fashion with which he had treated her all day. At least it was honest.

'See you five o'clock Friday,' he called after her as she drove off.

She waved, but quite determinedly resisted looking at him in the rear-vision mirror.

The clock on Harriet's bedside chest showed three a.m. She was still wide awake, a copy of *High-Rise* in her hands. She would be wrecked at school the next day, but she couldn't go to sleep just yet. She just *had* to read on.

The book was stunning. Simply stunning. Not only in its unexpected complexity of plot, but in its depth of characterisation, its sheer brilliance. Oh, yes, there were the usual—and much publicised—sex scenes. But they were emotional, rather than explicit. And never gratuitous.

Harriet finally put the novel away just before four, knowing that she couldn't possibly finish it that night with more than half the six hundred pages remaining. But she found it hard to get to sleep, her mind still whirling with the people in those pages, their lives, their emotions, their conflicts.

The main hero was so much more sympathetic than Brad's usual offering. He even had a conscience—of a sort—as he unwittingly uncovered the world of organised crime that lurked behind the façade of glamour on the Gold Coast. Harriet was especially touched by the growing relationship between the hero and Brigit, a waif-like stray he picked up off the streets one night, her life in tatters through drug addiction though she was only fifteen. With marked reluctance the hero allowed her to stay at his place and saw her through the pain of withdrawal. Naturally, she fell in love with her saviour, but while he was drawn to her he felt she was far too young, with her emotions confused by gratitude.

Of course the love-story was only a side-plot in the main thrust of the story but Harriet found its sensitivity very moving, displaying a side to Brad as a writer that had hitherto been hidden. Here was a man capable of at least expressing and conveying deep feelings. Very deep.

Harriet began to drift off to sleep, her own feelings strangely at odds now over this man. Prior to reading this latest book of his, she had really considered him an emotional light-weight, a man who would float through life like a gay barge along a river. All show. All on top. Superficial.

Now she wondered if that was so, if this highly entertaining and very sexy individual had more to him than met the eye.

She sighed as sleep snatched at the corners of her mind. So what if he had? she thought hazily. What difference would that ever make to her life...?

CHAPTER FIVE

'THERE'S the doorbell, Harriet. Shall I get it for you?'

Harriet grabbed her black patent leather clutch bag and fled her bedroom. 'No, no, I will,' she called back as she hurried along the hallway, her freshly shampooed hair swinging around her neck. She had visions of her mother coralling Brad on the front porch in order to extol the virtues of settling down permanently in a place like Valley's End with the right sort of wife.

Of course, this dinner date had inadvertently fed her mother's matrimonial hopes, more was the pity. Julia hadn't stopped speculating since Harriet had confessed where she was going and with whom, despite having delayed this unavoidable revelation till she had got home this Friday after school. It was amazing how far her mother's mind could leap in a little over an hour. She and Brad were practically on their honeymoon already!

'Have a nice time, dear,' her mother called out, surprising Harriet by staying firmly out of sight. From the sound of her voice she was still in the kitchen, not having come forward to spy from the proximity of the lounge-room. Was this another of her female ploys, the ones that came to her like water off a duck's back? A tactical retreat perhaps? Reverse psychology?

Harriet sighed and called something in reply, butterflies crowding her stomach as she approached the front door. She was both nervous and excited at the prospect of hearing Brad's opinion of her play.

She swept open the door, took one look at Brad and knew immediately that hearing about her play was not the sole reason for her excitement. She tried a deep breath and a cool smile, but they did nothing to stop the way her heart had begun to slam against her chest at the sight of him.

Her demand that he shave had certainly backfired on her. He'd been formidably attractive before in disreputable clothes, with stubbly chin. Now, clean-shaven and clad in smart cream linen trousers, a chocolate-brown shirt and tweedy jacket, he looked superb. His hair, too, had been snipped and tidied into a semblance of order, while still having a run-your-fingers-through-it appeal.

Harriet became embarrassingly aware that she was staring at him. But before any ghastly blush could give her away she found refuge in humour, grinning and waving a hand in mock salute to his appearance.

'Unpacked your good clothes at last, I see.'

He grinned back at her, his deep-set blue eyes dancing wickedly as they raked over her figure. 'I might say the same for you,' he returned.

Harriet was momentarily flustered by his frankly admiring gaze. She had done her best with her appearance, but still considered herself only passable, though even her mother had complimented her earlier on her choice of clothing. The black woollen suit, with its straight skirt and tailored jacket, was cut with more concession to the female form than her other suits, with a skirt length that barely brushed her knees and a jacket that nipped in at the waist before flaring out to flatter her slender hipline.

Brad's eyes, however, seemed mostly drawn to her cleavage, her meagre curves being shown to their best advantage by a black lace push-up bra and a black lace camisole. Normally Harriet wore this particular suit with a sensible blouse, and the jacket loose. Tonight, however, she had defiantly chosen the sexy underwear, then done up the jacket so that a small V of lace was on show. On a more voluptuous body this look would have been very sexy. Harriet knew she fell far short of that adjective, but she considered the outfit still looked quite sophisticated.

It also, it seemed, met with Brad's approval, which did nothing for her already erratic heartbeat. Common sense reminded her this was strictly a platonic date, but somehow her body wasn't listening.

'Did anyone ever tell you you scrub up pretty well, babe?' he drawled.

How odd that his use of that particular form of address could achieve what all her common sense could not. The wild heat his physical presence was evoking in her was immediately chilled. Her jaw clenched and she flicked a cold look his way. 'Not too many,' she replied bluntly.

He blinked a momentary confusion at her frosty answer, but quickly shrugged it off. His breezy, 'Come along, then, babe, we're off to see the little kitties,' had her wincing again, but she realised that here was a man who didn't let the feelings of his dates worry him for long. It was clear they were only there for his amusement, not his consternation.

Her suspicion that he might even try to bed her less than perfect body out of sheer boredom surfaced again, with her response to such a thing happening still irritatingly ambivalent. How could she consider letting such a womanising scoundrel touch her?

Her irritation grew as he conducted her to his car, settling her in with breezy smiles and outrageous flattery.

'Notice the clear cool night,' he remarked brightly. 'You have my prayers to thank for that...'

She almost chocked. Prayers? Him?

'I said to the Great Rainmaker in the sky, Not tonight, lord. Tonight I'm having to drive on a treacherous road with a beautiful woman beside me, so please, no rain, no other distractions.' He grinned down at her as he snapped her seatbelt into place.

Harriet dragged in a deep breath, hating herself for trembling when he brushed against her quite accidentally. Not that he noticed her reaction, for he had immediately swung her door shut then began striding around the front of the car. Still, it brought home to her how physically vulnerable to him she was, despite any irritation at his shallow ways. How on earth was she going to stop him if he decided seduction was on the menu for supper?

The answer was quite simple.

She would make sure such a situation could not develop.

Brad climbed in behind the wheel and fired the engine, with Harriet taking comfort from the fact that his flirtatious patter a moment ago meant little. That was just Brad, exercising his much-vaunted charm.

Her heart almost catapulted out of her chest when he unexpectedly leant over to run a finger across her forehead. 'Naughty girl,' he reprimanded. 'You'll get wrinkles if you keep frowning like that.'

She forced a light smile to her face, trying to hide the way her body had leapt at his fleeting touch. 'Is that so?' she tossed off casually. 'Maybe I'd look better with wrinkles. You've got a few and you look fine.'

'They're not wrinkles. They're laugh lines!'

She didn't doubt it—he laughed so much—but she made a face at him, nevertheless. 'Typical double set of standards,' she accused. 'Women get wrinkles. Men get laugh lines. You males get all the breaks.'

Brad chuckled, then eased the car away from the kerb and along the lane. 'Oh, I don't know. Women live longer.'

'But not so interestingly,' she shot back tartly.

He laughed again. 'Maybe... Well, babe, how about directing me to old Mrs Gallagher's place? I can't remember exactly where she lives.'

Harriet released her gritted teeth to say with admirably restrained patience, 'Take the next road on the left. And Brad, would you mind not calling me babe?'

'Oh? Why's that?' he said, darting a frowning glance over at her.

Her shrug was as inoffensive as her tone of voice. Or so she thought. 'I dislike it. I also dislike the indiscriminate use of sweetheart, honey, pet, love, dear and darling.'

'Hmm,' Brad murmured thoughtfully as he slowed at the end of the lane. 'What about swumpkin-dumpkins?'

Her chin snapped around so see him surveying her with a dead-pan expression. At least, it appeared to be till she glimpsed that wicked light dancing deep in his eyes.

'Typical male!' she rebuked. 'Making a joke over something a female finds infuriatingly demeaning. I call you Brad, don't I? Why not call me Harriet?'

'Aah... Now I understand. I have one of the enemy in my car. That dreaded individual, the women's liberationist!'

Harriet couldn't help it. She burst out laughing, for if there was one thing she wasn't it was a feminist. It was irony to a ridiculous extreme. Good heavens, didn't feminists believe a woman had the same rights as a man, including the right to good sex, with or without the benefit of a marriage contract? Yet here was this man—this *profligate*—accusing her—a *virgin*—of being...

She was laughing so hard she couldn't speak.

'Now, what did I say that was so damned funny?' he demanded.

She stopped laughing with a swallowing gulp. 'Nothing really. It's just that...that...' She couldn't really tell the truth, could she? 'It's just that every man I've ever gone out with has thought me rather... old-fashioned.'

That sardonic eyebrow lifted, and she could see the mental cogs ticking over in his brain. 'Oh? Why?' He threw her a knowing look. 'Because you don't come across on the first date?'

She blinked and swallowed again. Well, what did she expect? He was renowned for his blunt honesty.

'Something like that,' she choked out.

He made a face that showed what he thought of that type of man. Which again had its ironic side, considering. 'You won't have to worry about that with me,' he gruffed. 'You'll be delivered home safe and sound.'

This firm reassurance piqued what little ego she had left. 'Why is that, Brad?' she challenged. 'Aren't I your type?'

He frowned at her undeniably tart tone. 'That's rather a provocative question, isn't it, coming from one so... old-fashioned?'

Yes, it was. And Harriet quickly realised this once the madness subsided. Which it did with mortifying swiftness. Heat flooded her cheeks.

He turned his face towards her then, and their eyes met. It was the oddest look he gave her, one which, if she hadn't known better, she would have called anguished. She had the strongest feeling that he was tempted to say something for his lips parted, then pressed firmly back into grim silence as his eyes jerked back to the road. He even took a deep breath, as though gathering himself for a difficult task. But then, just as suddenly, his features relaxed, and his lips pulled back into a wry grin.

'Actually, Harriet, I don't think there is a type for me. I have liked and desired a great variety of women...' He hesitated, his face growing serious again, and Harriet held her breath. What on earth was he about to say? 'But I think I should be straight with you, before we find ourselves in a situation which I would most definitely regret.

'No doubt you are aware that I have been having a—relationship—with a certain lady in Sydney...'

Harriet nodded, her tongue dry in her mouth.

'We came to the parting of the ways recently. I am—and will always be—basically a loner. I like women. I like them as lovers, as well as friends. But I don't fall in love with them. I don't live with them. I don't *need* them, as such.' He darted an uncompromising glance her way. 'I do need sex at times, like most normal males, but, as you know, casual sex has its hazards. Which is why I choose to have some steady woman in my life rather than a different one here, a different one there. But I only take women to bed who know the score and whom I am confident will never fall in love with me. Do you understand what I'm saying, Harriet?'

Harriet tried to blank her mind to any astonishment his words produced, concentrating instead on what he actually *was* saying. Which was...what, exactly? He only became physically involved with women with whom he was emotionally uninvolved, and who were emotionally uninvolved with him?

'Is that what happened with Lydia Richmond, Brad?' she asked carefully. 'Did she fall in love with you?'

His laugh was surprisingly bitter. 'Good God, no! Dear Lydia could never fall in love with anyone. She's too in love with herself. No... When I told her where I was moving to she couldn't see herself commuting up here just for sex. Neither could I, so we called it quits.'

Harriet could no longer contain her dismay at the way Brad spoke of sex, so totally devoid of any association with love, or even liking. He was as amoral as she'd thought. What bothered her so much was why this didn't make her dislike him; why, in fact, she felt drawn to him and his almost throwaway lifestyle. Was it because it was so different from her own? Was it the old case of opposites attracting?

She didn't know, dropping her eyes and shaking her head in bewilderment.

'Quite,' Brad said drily. 'But give me credit for one thing, Harriet. I'm honest. And I'm giving you fair warning——'

Her eyes snapped up to his. 'And what do you mean by that?' she gasped.

He glared across at her. 'You're an intelligent woman, Harriet. But, I fear, a highly emotional one. You feel things... deeply. I have enough sense of honour left, I hope, not to tamper with your affection. Or your body.'

She stared back at him, hearing nothing but those last three words. 'I don't recall asking you to,' she snapped.

His eyes returned to the road. 'There is such a thing as body language, Harriet. Yours is beginning to disturb my equilibrium.'

'Oh, dear me,' she muttered sarcastically. 'How very unfortunate for you! Well, put your mind at rest, dear Mr Barrington, I'm not that desperate that I lust after every man I go out with. Neither would I dream of falling in love with a callous, hard-hearted bastard like you!'

He shocked her thoroughly by grinning quite unabashedly across at her. 'I'm delighted to hear that, Harriet. Delighted! Friends, then?'

She shook her head in total exasperation. 'My God, you would have to be the most egotistical, the most infuriating——'

'Left or right here, Harriet?' he cut in smoothly.

'What? Oh... left!'

'Right.'

'Not right, left! Oh, I see... You mean right meaning OK...' She sighed and touched a trembling hand to her forehead. This was turning into a nightmare. And the trouble was he was right about her body language. The madder she got at him, the more she wanted him. Her body was practically sizzling with rampant mental fantasies and barely held desire. It was all so crazy!

A line of logic crossed her mind that had a perverse kind of irony. If he felt sure she *wouldn't* fall in love with him, then he might make love to her. Of course, he would have to desire her back to do that, a factor that she had no real confidence about. Though he did seem the sort of man who found most women a turn-on. But was that all she wanted from him? Just sex? Her head seemed to be spinning with all sorts of thoughts, though her body didn't seem to have any doubts. Yes, yes, yes, it was saying to her.

'Not friends?' he sighed next to her.

She gave him a rueful look, but when he grinned across at her she melted, shaking her head more at herself and her own stupidity than at him. 'Friends,' she agreed.

'Good. It's this next place on the left, isn't it?' he said as he eased the powerful black car over on to the grass outside Mrs Gallagher's front fence.

Harriet nodded, thinking privately that she was mad to imagine she could keep this physical attraction in check if she kept on seeing Brad, even as a friend. This betraying 'body language' of hers could become embarrassing. It looked as if this dinner date would have to be their last one-to-one, but she wasn't about to spoil the rest of the evening by saying so just yet.

Mrs Gallagher was all aflutter when she opened the door to see who was calling. Harriet found the old lady's pleasure quite sad really, for it showed that she was not used to promised visits actually coming to fruition. Harriet vowed to come more often.

'The little darlings are doing very well,' the old woman gushed as she led them down the dim hallway through to an ancient kitchen, the kind that had copper pots hanging on the wall. *Real* copper pots.

'See?' She bent to where the four bundles of fur were lying in a basket in a corner near the warmth of the wood-fuelled stove. 'Yours is doing OK, young man,' she said, picking up the small white one and thrusting it into Brad's reluctant hands.

He held it away from his shirt, staring into its now opened blue eyes while it mewed its head off. He gave it a tentative pat with his spare hand, and the kitten abruptly began purring.

'See? She likes you,' Mrs Gallagher announced. 'It's a girl, you know. You'll have to have her desexed if you don't want litter after litter of kittens.'

Brad looked across at Harriet. 'Didn't I tell you?' he said soulfully. 'Females... Nothing but trouble.'

She shrugged, but said nothing. She wasn't going to buy into that one.

'She'll need to be taken home soon, though,' the old lady added. 'She's more timid than the others and won't do so well once I stop bottle-feeding her and they start lapping. The others will probably push her aside too much. She needs individual love and care or she'll be shy and frightened. Nothing worse than a frightened kitten. They soon learn to spit and claw, instead of purr.'

'You know a lot about cats, Mrs Gallagher, don't you?' Brad praised.

She beamed her pleasure at his compliment. 'Had cats all my life, young man. Complex creatures. But very worthwhile companions, once you get to understand them. Not pets, mind you. Cats will never be anyone's pet. They own you more than you own them.'

'Why don't you write a book on them?' Brad suggested. 'A sort of Cat Lovers' Companion, relaying all your own homespun advice.'

The faded blue eyes brightened with real enthusiasm. 'Do you think I could? I mean . . . I'd love to but who would publish it, or read it?'

'Lots of people, I would think. And I know plenty of bigwigs in the publishing industry. Just give the finished copy to me and I'll make sure it has a decent chance. Have it typed, though.'

'I can type,' she revealed, then her eagerness faded. 'But I haven't got a typewriter.'

'No trouble!' Brad exclaimed. 'I've got a perfectly good portable electric going to waste now that I've changed over to a word-processor. You can have it if you like.'

'Oh, but I couldn't, I mean that's much too generous of you, I——'

'Nonsense,' he cut in smoothly. 'It's just gathering dust where it is. I'll bring it down tomorrow.'

'Oh . . .' Her cheeks went pink, her eyes suddenly awash. 'Oh, dear . . .' She turned away and hurried across the room to snatch a handful of tissues from the box on the refrigerator, her sobs being muffled as she thrust them into her face.

Harriet felt a lump well up in her own throat. For a moment she could only stare at Brad, not knowing what to make of this man, this man who was unbelievably sweet and thoughtful to a little old lady, but who could callously announce that he only ever went to bed with women he felt no attachment to. He was certainly a creature of contradictions.

He looked totally bewildered by Mrs Gallagher's distress and turned to fix Harriet with an imploring look. 'I didn't mean to make her cry,' he rasped.

Harriet smiled understanding at him and moved forward to put tender hands on the old lady's shoulders. She didn't say a word but her comforting touch soon had the dear old thing pulling herself together.

'I'm sorry,' she said shakily, turning to face them with still-misty eyes. 'It's just that it's been a long time since...' She shook her head then drew her frail body up, proud and straight. 'You must let me show my gratitude, young man. Come to tea one night. And you too, Harriet.'

'We'd love to, wouldn't we, Harriet? But on one condition...'

Harriet was just as puzzled as Mrs Gallagher.

'You must stop calling me young man,' Brad elaborated with a cheeky grin. 'I am fast heading for the big four-O, and feel anything but young. I will answer to Brad. Or Barrington. Take your pick, dear lady.'

The old lady's returning smile was definitely coy, proving Harriet's theory that a smile and a few select words from this devil would charm *any* woman!

'Brad, then,' Mrs Gallagher simpered, and Harriet's eyes shot ceilingwards. She could just picture this tea right now. The best linen, the finest crockery, real silver cutlery. And the plumpest chicken in the yard. Nothing would be too good for 'Brad'. Tea, Harriet presumed, meant dinner, since most of Mrs Gallagher's generation tended to call the last meal of the day tea.

'Would next Saturday evening be suitable?' they were both asked. 'Around six?'

Harriet considered she was reasonably safe with Brad in Mrs Gallagher's company so six next Saturday was agreed upon, with little Brigit to be taken home afterwards.

Brad and Harriet were five minutes on their way to Coff's Harbour before she gave in to the desire to speak up. 'You would have to be the most contradictory man in the world, Brad Barrington.'

'Me? Come, now...in what way?'

'One moment you confess to having no time for emotional involvements, the next you spend time caring about the loneliness of an old lady you've only just met. Though don't think I didn't notice how you enjoyed charming her, as you do all the ladies. Present company excluded, of course,' she added drily.

He laughed. 'Keep that up, Harriet, and we'll be friends for life! As far as Mrs Gallagher is concerned, perhaps I just don't like seeing talent wasted. And the old lady has a definite talent for cats.'

'I don't believe it's as simple as that,' Harriet protested. 'I think you're deliberately misleading me about your character. Don't forget I've read *High-Rise*, which is not only the most entertaining novel I've ever read, but also one of the most moving. It has real emotion in those pages, Brad. Real emotion and real compassion. Both of which can only have come from the person who wrote it. You...'

She was aware that she had hit some nerve in him for he stiffened in his seat, his knuckles clenching around the steering-wheel.

'We all have emotions, Harriet,' he said at last, 'even the most base, and the most superficial.'

'Is that what you think you are, Brad?' she asked pensively. 'Base, and superficial? Or is that only what you want me to think?'

She was taken aback by the hard, angry glint in his eyes that sliced her way. 'Think what you damned well like. It won't change the truth.' He returned his attention to the road, which was winding its way steadily through the hills to the coast.

'Which is?' she pursued.

'I've already told you. I live my life for number one. Brad Barrington. Don't ever fool yourself into thinking otherwise.'

She fell silent at this.

'Changed your mind, have you?' he resumed, almost tauntingly. 'About our being friends?'

'Not at all.' Harriet could be incredibly stubborn.

'Then perhaps we should get down to the reason for this outing. Your play...'

Harriet lifted her head from where it had drooped a little, a surge of pride mixing with a dash of nerves. Gone were the days when men could defeat her totally. 'Very well. I suppose you think it's ghastly.'

'God, I detest false modesty.'

'False modesty! Why, you——?'

He lanced her with one of his sauciest grins, totally throwing her again. 'You bite well, Harriet.'

'And you're a snake!' she returned.

'I'm so glad you've finally realised.'

'Oh, I realised, Brad Barrington. I realised right from the start.'

'Splendid!' He looked ridiculously pleased with himself. 'Now, about your play...'

CHAPTER SIX

BRAD liked it. He actually liked it.

Though not unreservedly.

'I'm not a playwright,' he reminded Harriet. 'I can't advise you on matters of stage technique and such. But I feel qualified enough to criticise the writing itself, particularly regarding plot, characterisation and general construction.'

He proceeded to astound her by saying that he found her writing quite brilliant, the characters wonderfully depicted, the conflicts riveting, the dialogue superb. She was glowing all over by the time they reached Coff's Harbour and found a car park near the central shopping mall.

The crunch came over dinner, as Harriet was forking the last honeyed king prawn into her mouth. They had chosen a Chinese restaurant, tucked discreetly into an arcade, away from the mainstream of tourist crowds.

'Unfortunately,' Brad sighed, 'there is one definite problem with your play.'

Harriet's heart began sinking. 'Oh?'

'It would make a splendid period piece . . . set in the fifties perhaps. But as a modern-day story it runs into a real snag, since the premises on which you've based your conflicts are not credible today.'

Harriet gaped. 'Not credible?' How could real life not be credible?

He looked truly sorry at having to say what he was saying. 'Take your heroine, for instance, Henrietta... Now I know this is probably nit-picking, but how many girls these days are called Henrietta?'

'About as many as are called Harriet,' she shot back at him without thinking.

His returning glance was sharp. 'I thought you said the story wasn't autobiographical?'

Luckily, he couldn't detect her guilty blush in the reddish light that bathed the restaurant. 'It isn't,' she said with what she hoped was cool insistence. 'Go on. What else isn't credible?' She knew she was sounding quite curt but his criticism was patently unfair.

'Well, for one thing you have your heroine having had a lengthy relationship with this handsome, sexy guy called Grant, yet they've never got beyond a kiss. Now, Harriet, that doesn't make sense in this day and age, unless the bloke was gay, which he isn't, since he takes off with the heroine's female flatmate.'

Harriet bit her lip. Even she had found Graham's behaviour odd, putting it down later to her own lack of attractiveness. 'I can only say that's how it happened,' she defended. 'Remember, I told you it was partly based on a friend of mine's real-life experiences. The girl was rather plain, you see. And very inexperienced.'

'But still attractive enough to interest a very good-looking man into asking her to marry him. That just doesn't make sense, Harriet, unless the girl was an heiress, which she isn't. Not only that, you've made her twenty-six and still a virgin, despite having lived and worked in Sydney for several years. Now, unless she's the hunchback of Notre Dame, then, believe me, that's not credible!'

Of course she should have shut her mouth. She shouldn't have said a thing. But she was only human.

'Of course it's credible,' she hissed at him across the table. '*I'm* twenty-six and *I'm* still a virgin, dammit!'

The words hung in the air between them, the silence sizzling a lot more than the dish of Mongolian lamb that suddenly appeared. 'Your next dish, sir?'

The waitress placed it in the middle of the table and discreetly retreated after casting a quick glance at the two people gaping at each other, Brad in shock, Harriet in despairing humiliation.

She groaned, and dropped her eyes, only to jerk upright when Brad reached over to cover her shaking hand with his. 'Don't,' he murmured gently. 'Don't.'

She wasn't quite sure what he meant, but she did know it was meant kindly. Tears pricked at her eyes.

'Come on, eat up.' He withdrew his hand and spooned some of the steaming lamb on to her plate.

She did so, automatically, robotically, all the while hating herself and her big mouth. Why, oh, why had she let him goad her into admitting such a private thing? And why should the fact that she was a virgin be humiliating in the first place?

She finally accepted that it was because she hadn't *chosen* to remain a virgin. It had been thrust upon her due to her own lack of female desirability. No woman liked to think that a man had never wanted her.

'Would you like some dessert?' he offered when they had both finished the lamb.

She shook her head.

'Some Chinese tea perhaps?'

Again she shook her head. They'd had white wine earlier, and, in truth, she no longer wished to stay. The whole evening had been spoilt.

He sighed and gestured for the waitress. 'My check, please?'

It came directly and he gave a selection of notes which seemed to please the woman. A large tip, no doubt.

Harriet allowed herself to be led in silence back to the car. Brad climbed in beside her abject self, only to surprise her out of her introspective misery with an abrupt question. 'Tell me one thing,' he asked. 'This Grant, or whatever his real name is. You're still in love with him, aren't you?'

She turned dull eyes Brad's way, the memories of hurt filling them till they glazed over with the pain. 'His name is Graham,' she revealed, not even bothering to deny a thing. 'And, yes, I still love him.'

'And the gorgeous flatmate, Alexis. She was your best friend?'

'No...'

'Then she's a fictional character?'

'No.'

'Who, then?'

'Amanda.'

'Amanda?' He frowned as he searched his memory. 'Good God, you don't mean your sister, do you, the blonde on your father's desk?'

Harriet was suddenly past pain, past tears. 'Who else?' she said bitterly.

Brad's face was a picture of shock and pity. Oh, how she hated that pity!

'You mean to say your sister seduced your fiancé, then ran off to live with him?'

'Yes.'

'When?'

'You've read the play, Brad. Four years ago, when the heroine was twenty-two.'

'And Alexis—I mean Amanda—was only nineteen.'

'That's right.'

'That's disgusting!'

Harriet laughed. 'That's the pot calling the kettle black, isn't it, Brad? I would have thought such behaviour would hardly rate a rap over the knuckles in your world.'

She was not in any way prepared for what happened next. He grabbed her—quite roughly— dragging her towards him over the gear-lever. His eyes bored down into hers with real anger welling up in their depths. 'Don't you ever say that to me again, do you hear? I would never hurt anyone like that. *Never!* I take only what I'm offered, and give only what I'm capable of giving. I abhor what your sister did to you. Abhor it!'

He must have suddenly realised what he was doing, for his head rocked back to stare wide-eyed at the way his fingers were digging brutally into her flesh. With an anguished groan he released her, Harriet sagging back into the seat, her own eyes round with shock.

'I'm sorry, Harriet,' he muttered. 'Terribly sorry. I hope I didn't hurt you.' He slumped back into his own seat and closed his eyes, his chest rising and falling with long, shuddering breaths.

Harriet just sat there, still trembling, though more from the force of Brad's unexpected emotion than with fear. She had never dreamt he could react so passionately to anything!

'It's all right, Brad,' she said shakily. 'I...I shouldn't have said what I did. It was insulting.'

His eyes flicked slowly open and he slid a rueful look over at her. 'As if I don't need insulting every now and then... Oh, Harriet, what have I got myself into here with you? You touch my soul, do you know that? To think that a sister would do something so bloody awful to someone so fine... It's beyond the pale.'

Harriet shrugged off his pity, for she couldn't bear it, but the raw pain was still there in her face for Brad to see. 'I'm sure it isn't the first instance of its kind,' she dismissed. 'I've just had to live with it.'

'But you haven't, have you? Lived with it...'

'Of course I have,' she protested. 'I hardly think about it now.'

'Don't try to fool me, Harriet. I've read your play. Henrietta is nothing more than a bitter shell of a woman. And we both know now that Henrietta is you!'

'Big deal,' she muttered, finding sanctuary from her distress in a brittle offhandedness.

'Oh, Harriet, don't you see what you're doing to yourself, pretending to be hard when you're not?'

Harriet's temper flared as she saw she was about to be on the end of Brad's honest tongue again. But this time she would not endure his saying things to her over something he knew nothing about.

'I don't think——'

'For God's sake shut up and listen for once in your life, will you?'

She gasped, her mouth opening and closing a couple of times before pressing shut into a thin angry line.

'You need someone to take you in hand, Miss Prickly Pear. Someone who'll steer you in the right direction to get over dear Graham and Co.'

'And what's that?' she scorned. 'Filling my life with passing sexual encounters? That is your recipe for a fulfilled, happy life, isn't it, Brad?' Her voice was heavy with sarcasm. 'But of course I have to remember only to go to bed with men I *don't* love, and who definitely don't love me, isn't that it?'

His glance was withering. 'I wouldn't recommend it for one so young and sensitive. But some sort of sex life would be a damned sight more healthy than what you've been doing for the last four years: pining after someone who doesn't deserve you, wasting your youth on a dead dream, a ghost, a fantasy of your romantic soul. This Graham never loved you, will never love you. At least be honest and find some pleasure in life, and if that means with another man, or men, then why not?'

'And whom would you suggest, Mr. Know-It-All? I don't exactly see a long line of beddable males clamouring their way to my door! I'm not Amanda, you know.'

He gave her a long, considering look. 'So that's your beef, is it? Poor little Harriet can't compete with her beautiful sexy sister so she throws up the sponge and develops an acid tongue, just in case some unfortunate male does happen to stray her way and *dares* to take an interest in her. Which of course couldn't possibly happen, because she's so plain and undesirable.'

She glared at him, hating him for his cruel truths. 'Well, I am, aren't I?' she threw back.

'No.'

'Liar! I have nothing going for me and you know it. No face, no figure, no sex appeal whatsoever. There's no point in denying it. I know! I've had to live with it for years. No dates, no boyfriends, no second glances, no nothing!'

'What about Graham?' Brad reminded her.

'Well, what about him? He ended up with Amanda, didn't he?'

'But he started off with you, Harriet,' Brad argued. 'Why?'

She shrugged. 'God only knows.'

'I think I know why,' he offered.

She was quite startled. And showed it.

'Would you like me to tell you? Or will you accuse me of lying again?'

She frowned. 'I'll listen,' she said at last. 'You're usually honest. Uncompromisingly so,' she finished drily.

He laughed. 'That's good, then. It will make my job of convincing you how wrong you are about yourself so much easier.'

She shook her head, wondering if he was really going to be honest. Or if his pity for her would make him compromise his usual frankness.

'You're going to be difficult, aren't you?' he said, catching her sceptical look. 'Difficult and stubborn. But that's all right. That's one of the things I like about you. That and your lack of hypocrisy, and your inability to manipulate. You might be misguided, but at least you're up front, Harriet, which is a good start.'

She sighed. 'I'm not sure I know what you're talking about now, Brad.'

'You will, Harriet, in time...'

She gave a nervous laugh. 'You sound as if this could take all night.'

'Oh, it will,' he said matter-of-factly. 'Definitely.'

'I don't see why it——'

'Please stop interrupting, Harriet. Now that *is* one bad habit of yours, always wanting your say.'

'There you go again!' she burst out irritably. 'If a man has his say, he's assertive; if a woman does, she's an aggressive bitch.'

Brad glared at her, pressing his lips tightly together in anger. With an exasperated grunt he twisted back to face the front, then reached to turn on the engine.

'What...what are you doing?' she stammered. 'I thought you were going to tell me why Graham asked me to marry him?'

'I was,' he growled back at her, revving the engine and reversing out of the car park. 'But I've changed my mind. You're not in a receptive mood just at the moment.'

'But I...I...'

'Now, be a good girl, Harriet, and give that mouth of yours a rest, will you? You'll be needing it later on.'

'What on earth——?'

He cut her off with a dry, forceful look and put his foot down on the accelerator. 'Look, you know the drive back to Valley's End is a bastard and I'd like to make it in under an hour. I've decided it is futile to continue any discussion about your character until I've got a little something out of the way.'

A prickle ran up and down her spine. 'A little something? What little something?'

One eyebrow lifted in what seemed like slow motion and his eyes slid slowly to that black lace at her breasts. 'Your virginity, Harriet. What else?'

CHAPTER SEVEN

'What . . . what did you say?' Harriet gasped.

'You heard me, Harriet.'

She stared at Brad, but he kept his eyes straight ahead, his attention on the winding road.

'My God, who do you think you are, saying something like that?'

He gave her the benefit of a quick glance, stunning her with the genuine warmth it conveyed. 'Your friend, I hope.'

She swallowed. 'F. . . friends don't go round offering to go to bed, just because one of them is . . . hasn't . . . Oh, you know what I mean! The idea is perfectly ludicrous.'

'I think it's perfectly sensible. Who better to trust one's body to than a friend?'

Angry eyes flashed at him. 'How typically Bohemian of you, Brad Barrington! And how many women have you offered this version of friendship to over the years?'

He laughed. 'Quite a few, actually. But you're my first virgin.'

'I should have known! Virgins would hardly be your style, would they?'

'Well, they haven't exactly fulfilled my criterion in the past.'

'Which is that they shouldn't become emotionally involved with you, right?'

'Right.'

'So now that you know I'm still in love with Graham I qualify, is that it?'

'Of course.'

She huffed her exasperation. 'Even though I'm not up to scratch, looks-wise?'

He slanted a wry smile her way. 'You'll do, Harriet. You'll do.'

'God! Am I supposed to be flattered by that lukewarm compliment?'

He chuckled. 'Would you believe me if I said I thought you positively delicious and that I've been lusting after you ever since you set those big brown eyes on me last week?'

'Hardly.'

'Well, then, be thankful for small mercies.'

'You do wonders for my ego.'

'I could if you'd let me.'

'Meaning?'

'Meaning I could tell you how much I fancy tall slender women with long, long legs, how I just adore thick glossy hair like yours, how I find the chip you wear on your shoulder positively challenging, but, more to the point, how I'm also finding it very hard not to steer this car over to the side of the road and ravish you right here and now!'

'Huh!' she scoffed. 'As if I'd let you anyway.'

'Harriet, darling...' his eyes raked over her body with lecherous intent '...you couldn't stop me.'

She sniffed her scorn, lifting her chin and tossing back her hair. 'You might be a lot of things, Brad Barrington, but you're not a rapist. Your macho male ego couldn't stand having to take a woman by force. You fancy yourself the ultimate seducer!'

His laughter this time was rollicking. 'Really? Oh, Harriet, how well you don't know me!'

'Laugh all you like. I know I'm right.'

He grinned across at her. 'You think so?'

She shot him a scornful look. 'You know damned well you never have any trouble worming your way into a woman's bed.'

'What about yours?'

'What about mine? It's at my parents' place. Something tells me you're not driving back there!'

And so it went on, all the way back to Valley's End, Brad making some outrageous remark, and Harriet coming back with an equally provocative retort. Her blood ran hotter and hotter, though whether from outrage or not she wasn't sure. Their bantering had the flavour of verbal foreplay, she suspected, for at no time did she deny his pronouncement that he was going to take her to bed.

If anything she confirmed her agreement by saying at last, 'I might get pregnant, you know.'

He didn't reply for a second or two, then slid a reproachful look her way. 'I wouldn't let that happen to you, Harriet.'

'Oh, yes, I forgot,' she derided. 'We have a man of the world here. No nasty complications for him like a pregnancy. Heavens, how could I be so naïve as to even think such a thing!'

His sigh was deep. 'You know, Harriet, the more you talk like this, the more I realise you need a man very badly.'

She fell silent at that, her heart having twisted at the gentleness of his words. It reminded her forcibly that for all his outrageous behaviour Brad possessed a genuine streak of kindness.

He's doing this out of pity, the voice of brutal truth told her. He doesn't desire you. He pities you...

Harriet stuffed a clenched fist in her mouth to stop her despair finding voice. She turned her head and blinked misty eyes into the night, only then realising that their arrival at Brad's farm was imminent.

'You've gone suspiciously quiet,' Brad said as he negotiated the last curve before the house came into view.

'What time is it?' she asked, needing to turn the conversation away from herself.

He pulled the car up in front of the house before glancing at his watch. 'Ten-fifteen. Why? Do you have to be home at a certain time?'

'No.' A shiver ran up her spine. 'No,' she repeated. She turned suddenly panicky eyes towards him but he was already out of the car and on his way around to her side.

'Your hands are freezing,' Brad commented as he helped her out of the car.

She pulled away from him and hurried ahead, up the steps on to the veranda where she turned to send wide eyes over the valley. 'There's a mist rolling in,' she said with far more composure than she was feeling. Nerves were crowding her stomach but there was no going back now. For, despite all her protestations, Harriet knew Brad was right. She needed to do this. And she might never have another opportunity.

He came up the steps to stand in front of her, a frown on his wide forehead. 'Stop running away, Harriet,' he murmured softly. 'I'm not going to hurt you.' His hands reached up to curl over her shoulders and he drew her gently against his chest. She shivered, then sagged into his body, sliding her arms up under his jacket and around his broad back. He felt strong and warm. Welcoming. It was like coming home after being away for a long, long time.

'You don't have to go through with this, you know,' he whispered into her hair. 'If you're really appalled at the idea...'

She pulled back, her mind quite clear, any lingering doubts gone. 'No... I *want* to,' she said quite passionately. 'It's just that...'

One corner of his mouth lifted wryly. 'Just what?'

Big brown eyes searched his handsome face. 'I would hate to think you were taking me to bed out of pity.'

Something glimmered deep in his eyes, and his smile widened. Why had her comment amused him?

'Be assured, Harriet, men rarely take women to bed out of pity.' Smiling eyes caressed her worried ones. 'No, my little inferiority complex, I want you. I really want you. And if you dare ask why I'm going to turn you over my knee and smack that saucy little backside of yours.' He lifted his eyebrows up and down in exaggerated lechery. 'Hmm, that idea has possibilities!'

She didn't know whether to blush, or laugh. He was incorrigible! A reluctant smile tugged at her lips.

'Aah...now that's what I like,' he enthused. 'A happy mouth.'

His kiss took her by surprise. He captured her lips while parted, covering them fully with his own before slipping his tongue inside. She clung to him in stunned fright as her body rippled with excitement, her fingertips digging into his shoulder-blades. It was just as well she had a tight hold on him for when his tongue started thrusting deep into her mouth Harriet's knees almost gave way. Her head began to swim, the blood in her temples swirling in heated circles.

His hands slid along her shoulders and up her throat, his thumbs resting along her jawline while his fingers splayed up into her hair. He kept re-arranging their mouths in new positions, noses first this side then the other, as though searching for some better position in which he could fuse his mouth even closer to hers.

Strange whimpering sounds kept escaping from Harriet's throat whenever Brad abandoned her mouth for longer than a second. She was also fast relinquishing the role of surprised innocent. She was pressing her body into his, her small firm breasts squashed agonisingly flat, her soft stomach moulding around his hardness in flagrant invitation.

Oddly enough, while all this was going on her mind seemed to be working on some weirdly detached level which sought to examine what was happening.

AN IMPORTANT MESSAGE
FROM
THE EDITORS OF HARLEQUIN®

Dear Reader,

Because you've chosen to read one of our fine romance novels, we'd like to say "thank you"! And, as a **special** way to thank you, we've selected <u>four more</u> of the **books** you love so well, **and** a Victorian Picture Frame to send you absolutely *FREE!*

Please enjoy them with our compliments...

Editor,
Presents

Dianne Moeson

P.S. And <u>because</u> we value our customers, we've attached something extra inside ...

EDITOR'S
FREE GIFT SEAL
THANK YOU

PEEL OFF SEAL AND PLACE INSIDE

HOW TO VALIDATE
YOUR
EDITOR'S FREE GIFT
"THANK YOU"

1. Peel off gift seal from front cover. Place it in space provided at right. This automatically entitles you to receive four free books and a lovely pewter-finish Victorian Picture Frame.

2. Send back this card and you'll get brand-new Harlequin Presents® novels. These books have a cover price of $2.99 each, but they are yours to keep absolutely free.

3. There's no catch. You're under no obligation to buy anything. We charge nothing—ZERO—for your first shipment. And you don't have to make any minimum number of purchases—not even one!

4. The fact is thousands of readers enjoy receiving books by mail from the Harlequin Reader Service®. They like the convenience of home delivery...they like getting the best new novels months before they're available in stores...and they love our discount prices!

5. We hope that after receiving your free books you'll want to remain a subscriber. But the choice is yours—to continue or cancel, anytime at all! So why not take us up on our invitation, with no risk of any kind. You'll be glad you did!

6. Don't forget to detach your FREE BOOKMARK. And remember...just for validating your Editor's Free Gift Offer, we'll send you FIVE MORE gifts, *ABSOLUTELY FREE!*

YOURS FREE!
*This lovely Victorian pewter-finish miniature is perfect for displaying a treasured photograph–and it's yours **absolutely free**–when you accept our no-risk offer!*

THE EDITOR'S "THANK YOU" FREE GIFTS INCLUDE:

▶ Four BRAND-NEW romance novels
▶ A pewter-finish Victorian picture frame

PLACE
FREE GIFT
SEAL
HERE

YES! I have placed my Editor's "thank you" seal in the space provided above. Please send me 4 free books and a Victorian picture frame. I understand I am under no obligation to purchase any books, as explained on the back and on the opposite page.

106 CIH AKXQ (U-H-P-09/93)

_____
NAME

_____
ADDRESS   APT.

_____
CITY   STATE   ZIP

Thank you!

THE HARLEQUIN READER SERVICE®: HERE'S HOW IT WORKS

Accepting free books puts you under no obligation to buy anything. You may keep the books and gift and return the shipping statement marked "cancel." If you do not cancel, about a month later we will send you 6 additional novels, and bill you just $2.24 each plus 25¢ delivery and applicable sales tax, if any.* That's the complete price, and—compared to cover prices of $2.99 each—quite a bargain! You may cancel at any time, but if you choose to continue, every month we'll send you 6 more books, which you may either purchase at the discount price...or return at our expense and cancel your subscription.

*Terms and prices subject to change without notice. Sales tax applicable in N.Y.

Graham's kisses never affected you like this, a puzzled voice recalled.

And they hadn't. They'd been soft and sweet and romantic, rather like sipping a warm drink on a cool evening. This was like a shot of whisky, burning its path down her throat then hitting her stomach with the devastating force of a bomb, the after-shocks mushrooming up through her chest to explode in her head, scattering any sense of conscience to the four winds.

It doesn't matter that Brad doesn't love me, she told herself as her body quivered and melted with wild desire. He likes me and he wants me. I know he does, I can *feel* it.

It was amazing how intoxicating that realisation was, for it proved beyond a doubt that he hadn't been lying about wanting her.

Quite unexpectedly he stopped, pulling his face back to stare down into her madly dilating eyes.

'A *virgin*, Harriet?' He was breathing heavily. 'God! How come?'

'I . . . I . . .'

He sealed her panting stammer with a fleeting kiss. 'No need to answer,' he said with a sigh. 'That was a rhetorical question. But I think some breathing-space is called for. If things keep going at this pace you might find the outcome quite unsatisfactory.'

Harriet didn't agree. She wished he hadn't stopped, hadn't spoken. It would have been much better if he had swept her up into his arms, carried her inside and did the deed, post-haste. Then she wouldn't have had time to worry about what he thought of her body or lack of experience. This way...

Her face contorted into a grimace at the thought of his undressing her with slow deliberation.

'Cold feet again, Harriet?' he teased.

Her chin lifted. 'Of course not!'

He laughed. 'You have courage, Prickly Pear. I'll give you that.'

'Will you stop calling me that?' she protested.

'Can't. You've ruled out all my other terms of endearment.'

'I would hardly call Prickly Pear a term of endearment!'

'Ah, but it is. It certainly is. But I will bow to your wishes. OK, come along...*comrade*...I have a nice bottle of port that's just dying to be opened. We'll light the fire in the lounge-room and relax, shall we?'

Comrade? She almost laughed at that one. Dear capitalist Brad was as far removed from socialism as one could get. She smiled at him in wry amusement as he led her inside the house.

Less than an hour later Harriet had to admit that she *was* relaxed, surprisingly so. Sitting, watching a fire was always cosy, and Brad had pulled two of the armchairs closer to the hearth for them to sit in, with a small table in between to hold the port and the glasses.

Brad was semi-reclining in the larger of the two chairs, his jacket discarded, long legs extended towards the flames. Harriet was curled up in hers, heels tucked under, her tight skirt riding up dangerously high to reveal bare knees and thighs.

Her tights and shoes rested neatly beside the fire.
Brad's suggestion. One which she had neither
dared to question nor refuse. All the less clothes to
take off later, she supposed with surprising
resignation.

The bottle of port was on its last legs, its effect
spreading a warm glow through Harriet's body.
Conversation had died down all of a sudden and
Brad slid a languorous look her way. 'How about
coming over here into my chair?' he drawled.

Refusing to resort to coyness at this stage, she
did as he asked, her heartbeat revving up again as
she tried to arrange herself on his lap. It was a bit
of a squash till Brad flipped her legs over the right
arm of the chair, pushing the small table back out
of harm's way. Her arms automatically snaked
around his neck for support.

For an interminably long time he just stared into
her eyes.

It was arousing, that penetrating gaze. Arousing
and disturbing. What was he thinking behind those
half-closed lids? Was he wondering what in the hell
he was doing here? Or was he remembering other,
far sexier partners?

A mad impulse took over and she leant forward
to press her mouth against his. She even darted her
tongue forward to run it nervously over his lips. He
startled her by gripping her shoulders and jerking
her away, glaring at her for a second before pulling
her slowly back against him, his mouth quickly
imprinting on hers who was going to be the boss
in this encounter. Strong hands cradled her face,
then slid up into her hair, massaging her throbbing

scalp with exquisite skill. When the kiss finally ended, Harriet was left limp and quivering. She presented her parted lips for yet more, but he declined, holding her away from him and staring at her once again with oddly angry eyes.

Why was he angry? Harriet's dazed brain puzzled. Why?

Harriet was suddenly swamped with the awful feeling that maybe Brad needed a strong emotion like anger in order to whip up the necessary passion to make love to her. She had too long been spurned by men to seriously believe he was compelled to this end by desire for her. He'd had plenty of opportunity before tonight to make any desire on his part evident. Yet he hadn't even tried to kiss her.

Still... She did believe him when he said he wasn't doing it out of pity. He was so brutally honest that she just had to believe him. All she could think of was that he might be one of those men who liked the thought of being her first lover, liked playing the role of master to her inexperience. Perhaps that was why he'd been annoyed at her trying to take the initiative. Maybe it was a matter of power. Yes, that was it, she decided. It had to be. There was certainly no love or deep caring involved.

Harriet felt a twisting inside her heart, but steadfastly ignored it. She had given up expecting much on any personal level ages ago. To have this gorgeous, sexy man make love to her, no matter what the reason, was an unexpected bonus.

She was startled when he abruptly reached up to draw her arms away from his neck, and yet the anger she had glimpsed had gone, his feelings hidden behind a blank mask. He began undoing the buttons of her jacket, holding her suddenly wide eyes with this new unreadable gaze, his busy fingers not stopping till the last button had given way. His eyes skimmed her creamy flesh, flashing briefly as they lingered on the faint shadow between her breasts. He dragged in a single deep breath which he exhaled very slowly.

'And you think you're plain,' he murmured thickly. 'Oh, silly, silly Harriet...' He peeled the jacket back from her shoulders, eased it down off her arms and threw it over to her empty chair.

An involuntary shiver ran up and and down her bare arms.

'Not cold, are you?' he asked.

She shook her head, not trusting her voice.

He rubbed her arms up and down, bringing a rash of goose-bumps, all the while looking her over. She felt her nipples push hard against her bra; felt, in fact, her entire breasts swell till they were painful orbs of flesh fighting their confinement. She was torn between relief and embarrassment when Brad pulled the camisole free of her skirt then slipped his hand up her back, unsnapping the strapless bra and drawing it away. It joined the discarded jacket.

Harriet scooped in a quivering breath, making her even more shockingly aware of those rock-like points jutting now through thin black lace. Any qualms about the size of her breasts receded, for, indeed, they neither felt not looked small at that moment. Instead, their swollen curves were vibrating with an aching desire to be touched.

But Brad's hands had returned to the armrests of the chair, only his eyes giving her the benefit of their attention. But oh, those eyes. They told her things she could barely believe. They danced and smouldered, they hungered and devoured. And it could only be for her, for Harriet.

Heat claimed her body, rushing to inflame her nerve-endings and bring a rosy glow to her skin. She sat, quivering with longing, witnessing his unbelievable desire with barely held patience. Why, then, didn't he touch her? Why?

His right hand finally moved to tip her sideways, her feet fluttering upwards as she felt herself over-balance. She gasped with fright but he was there to catch her with his other arm, enfolding her into the curve of his shoulder. She had barely caught her breath when this hand moved again, this time to her right breast, the fingertips brushing lightly across the tense nipple. It sprang even harder against the lace, if that was possible, Harriet's stomach twisting into a knot when the centre of his palm began rotating over it in ecstatically pleasurable circles.

She couldn't believe the sensations coursing through her body. She was stirred in places that were nowhere near her breasts. Her entire body, in fact, began going up in flames. She wanted to moan, to writhe against that tormenting hand, but she kept still and silent, biting her bottom lip in a sweet silent agony.

Then, when she thought she would scream with the unbearable torture of it all, he kissed her, her whole body shuddering with relief as the hand moved to lie in peaceful possession over her other breast.

It was a different kiss from the first two. It was slow and initially much less demanding, with his tongue tracing her mouth for ages before dipping gently between her panting lips. But then, imperceptibly, the kiss deepened, and the soothing hand began to move, the thumb and forefinger playing with this next nipple till it was as excruciatingly tender as the other, but oh, so responsive. Once again she began to feel little tugs down there between her thighs, as though her muscles were clenching then releasing. A void seemed to be opening up in her body, a void that needed to be filled, quite desperately.

Harriet wanted Brad's body inside her with an urgency that was so compelling she was awestruck. Was this how it would have been with Graham? came the wide-eyed, wondering thought.

She wrenched her mouth away from Brad's, staring at him in shock at the way her mind had instinctively reacted to that thought. No, it had screamed back at her. No, it wouldn't have!

He saw her astonishment and tried to soothe it, taking his hand from her breast and stroking her cheek. 'It's all right, Harriet. It's all right. I'm probably going too fast for you...'

That's not it, she wanted to tell him. That's not it!

She stared at him and tried to understand why she should feel more strongly for him in a physical sense than she had for Graham. It didn't make sense. Graham had been her knight in shining armour, her prince, her dream come true. Graham was equally handsome, and infinitely more romantic than this man. Was it just Brad's practised sexual expertise she was responding to?

'Stop thinking, Harriet,' he advised softly. 'Stop thinking... Close your eyes and feel. Kiss me, Harriet.'

A soft despairing cry broke from her throat as she bent to his will, quickly falling victim to the seducing power of his lips and tongue. It was so easy to forget everything with her eyes closed and his mouth on hers, everything except this growing, nagging, insidious longing to be as one.

Harriet's breath caught in her throat when his hand skimmed down her body to ease between her thighs, briefly caressing the soft flesh there before sliding upwards. She tried to ignore its tantalising travels, giving her whole attention to their kiss, but it was difficult. Downright impossible once Brad abruptly lifted his lips from hers.

'We'll have to dispense with these too,' he murmured, plucking at the lace of her bikini briefs.

Oh, God...

She kept her eyes squeezed tightly shut while he helped her wriggle out of her underwear, though oddly enough he did nothing about her black woollen skirt. It had ridden up to a ridiculous level, straddling her hips, the silk lining sliding against her bare buttocks. She gasped with shock when his hand returned to explore her quite intimately, stroking her flesh into a liquid heat. Any sense of embarrassment was distracted by his kissing her again, his tongue darting repeatedly inside her mouth in synchronisation with his other, much more shattering invasion.

Harriet was by now far from relaxed. She was a mass of electrified nerves and growing tension. Alternately she wanted to open her body up to his ministrations and then, with savage defiance, she would force his touch to still.

He only laughed at this, a deep sexy laugh, but in the end he withdrew his hand, sliding it up her arm to find the thin black strap of the camisole. He eased it off her left shoulder then rolled it down till the lace fell from her breast. With a twisting motion he moved himself slightly to one side, the arm under her shoulders shifting to lower her head and lift her chest.

She knew what he was going to do, but still she wasn't ready for it, wasn't ready for the way it felt when he sucked the tortured peak into his mouth. She bit her lip, and pressed her thighs even tighter together. Yet this only seemed to make things worse. The need, the compulsion to beg him to take her was growing with each second. But she couldn't bring herself to be so bold, so wanton. She tried to relax her legs but they had a mind of their own. They moved restlessly, her hips writhing against his thighs.

He muttered something low under his breath, then with an abrupt, almost violent movement swept her up and carried her from the room, striding down the hallway and into the darkened front room. This was it, she realised, dry-mouthed, as he laid her down into the softness of a quilt. There was no turning back now.

But he moved away, his desertion surprising her till he started pulling the curtains back from the windows. The moonlight alleviated the blackness of the room, its filtered rays falling across the bare floor and up on to where she was lying on a double bed.

Harriet's breath caught in her throat when he turned and just stood there, staring down at her, his face and body in shadow. He looked even more overwhelmingly sexy in silhouette, she thought. Larger. More dominating. Incredibly male.

Her heart began to pound even louder, so loud that she thought he must hear it in the quiet stillness of the room. But along with her arousal came a prickling of fear, fear of what was to come, fear that she would somehow make a fool of herself, that he would find her gauche and boring. But worst of all fear that she herself might find the experience painful, or awful, or simply disappointing.

What...what are you doing over there?' she rasped when he stayed where he was.

Did he smile? She couldn't see, with his face in shadow like that, but it seemed his voice smiled as he said, 'Getting myself under control, Harriet. Getting myself under control...'

'Oh.' She swallowed, watching him with her heartbeat fluttering as he walked slowly across and around the foot of the bed. His eyes moved into the moonlight by the time he reached her, and when he bent down to kiss her Harriet was slightly dismayed to see those familiar wicked lights dancing in his eyes. She could not dismiss the thought that this was just another sexual jaunt for him, a pleasant way to pass an evening. Whereas for her it was a momentous occasion, a never to be repeated experience.

But as quickly as these dampening thoughts descended they disappeared, scattered by the seductive power of his kiss. Who could think properly when his lips and tongue were in play over the responsive surfaces of her mouth?

'You look very appealing lying there in this light,' he whispered when finally he straightened. 'Even more appealing, I would think, without some of these clothes.' And he began to slowly unzip and remove her skirt, his fingers sure and steady.

'Hmm...delicious,' came his murmur of approval once the task was completed.

Harriet couldn't even summon up a blush, for she found she liked his hot eyes on her semi-nakedness, liked the way the lace camisole flattered that area of her body she felt deficient.

'But I'd like this off as well,' Brad insisted, whipping this last vestige of modesty off over her head before she could object.

Now she dived under the quilt and he laughed. 'Such sudden shyness,' he teased, his hands already on the buttons of his own shirt.

'Perhaps I'm just cold,' she flung back at him, heart racing.

'And I'm Mother Goose!' He tore open the shirt, exposing a magnificently hairy chest.

'Hardly,' she muttered, her eyes feasting on his sheer male beauty.

Trousers joined the shirt. Then his briefs.

Harriet decided then and there that whatever his reason for making love to her was it was very effective.

The mattress dipped madly when he sat down and removed his shoes and socks, rolling Harriet into the centre of the bed. When Brad joined her under the quilt she kept rolling right into him.

Harriet stiffened at the alien feel of being in bed with a naked man, a naked *aroused* man. It was one thing to imagine how it might feel, quite another to suddenly have his throbbing hardness lying against her. She lifted one knee to place on Brad's thigh, thinking this would temporarily distance her from his disturbing virility, only to find her change of position now had it pulsating against her.

'Don't *do* that!' Brad muttered.

'I'm not doing anything,' she gasped. 'It's *you*!'

But it wasn't long before it *was* Harriet. Slowly, tentatively, she moved again, seeking that electric sensation that had charged through her when his quivering flesh had made contact with her. And there it was again, exciting her, enslaving her. She moved again, and again.

'Harriet, stop,' he choked out.

'I can't,' she panted, her tongue thick in her throat. 'Can't...'

'Hell,' he groaned, and, grasping her upper arms, rolled her over till she was pinned beneath him.

She responded by centring her molten need around him and arching her back.

No man could have resisted such a temptation. Brad certainly couldn't. Even so he eased into her with amazing control.

Harriet gasped, both from surprise and pleasure. There was no pain. No discomfort. Only the exquisite sensation of the void having been filled. But the nagging ache had only been partly assuaged, there remaining a mad desire to rush ahead towards total satisfaction. She placed her arms around his neck, moving her lower body in a frenzied fervour.

An animal sound rumbled deep in Brad's throat. 'God, Harriet, give me a break, will you?'

'How?' she gasped.

'Slow and steady wins the race, my impatient minx. Slow and steady...'

He slid wide-spread hands under her buttocks, his firm grasp forcing her writhing flesh into immobility before he began to move. Slowly and steadily.

Harriet's breathing grew shallow and fast, her mind struggling to assess if what she was feeling was still pleasure. Or sheer torture. She wanted him to move more quickly, wanted desperately to move with him. But he held her in an iron grasp, her lower back half lifted off the bed so that she had no traction.

Eventually his rhythm picked up, but oddly enough this didn't satisfy Harriet. All it did was propel her on to another level of sensation and tension even more distressing than before. Her mind whirled, her breathing becoming so frantic that she feared it was squeezing the very life from her lungs.

Beads of perspiration broke out on her forehead. She was hot, terribly hot. Too hot. When he bent to kiss her she wrenched her mouth from his, gasping for breath.

Any remaining pleasure soon became panic. She felt as though she were having a nightmare, dreaming an elusive dream that kept flitting through her brain then dashing off to a distant horizon. She was never going to reach it, for the closer she seemed to get, the further the horizon withdrew.

She gave a whimpering, distressed sob, her head thrashing from side to side in fevered frustration. 'Stop . . . oh, stop,' she cried.

Brad stopped immediately, dragging in several deep, ragged breaths as he sought to bring control over his obviously impassioned body. He even withdrew, reaching a gentle hand up to stroke the hair back from her sweat-streaked face.

'I'm sorry, Harriet, sorry,' he rasped. 'I got carried away. Hell, I should have known how this might affect me.' He sighed, then bent to kiss her forehead, her eyes, her nose. 'It's all right, Harriet. Try to relax. You're far too tense.' He let go his hold on her buttocks, rubbing her flesh with warm, soothing hands. 'I wasn't hurting you, was I?'

'No . . . not really.' She blinked, her mind confused by his words. Perhaps he meant that it had been a long time since he had had a woman. Why else would he be so affected?

He kissed the worry from her face then pulled back to lick her breasts, tonguing the sensitive peaks with soft, sweet licks. Then he sank back into her, telling her all the while how beautiful she was, how much he wanted her, keeping his movements much more gentle and controlled.

And his words helped. His gentleness helped. They brought a sense of loving and caring to what he was doing that seemed to release Harriet from her prison of pained tension. Soon she was soaring on a different type of journey. She was able to give as well as receive, to move with him, to feel that they were making love, not just having sex. She pressed her lips to his shoulders, his neck, his face. Her hands roved his back, moulding his muscles, then sliding up to play with his hair.

Harriet's climax took her by surprise. It started through her body on a deceptively low-key note, like a slow, rippling wave, which subtly took hold, rolling on and on with ever-increasing force, growing larger and larger till it was a tidal wave of enormous power. She grew light-headed under its escalating force, her heartbeat ceasing, her chest tightening as it held her high on the swell for a few breathless seconds before hurling her headlong into the deep, crashing and curling over her, convulsing her flesh with a battery of tumultuous feelings.

Brad's guttural cry of pleasure sent an exultant thrill through Harriet, his shuddering release prolonging the sharply exquisite delights that were ricocheting throughout her body. 'Oh, Brad,' she cried, clasping him to her when his exhausted body collapsed on top of hers. 'Thank you... Thank you...'

He stayed where he was for a full minute, his breathing ragged, before rolling from her to lie on his side. Sighing, he propped himself up on one elbow while his free hand touched her lightly and gently across tender lips. 'Thank you, too,' he murmured back.

'Brad... I never dreamt... It was so wonderful... *You* were wonderful...' She snuggled into him, closing her eyes as a seeping languor invaded her entire being. She yawned before she could stop herself.

His laughter was low and warm as he bestowed a light kiss on top of her head. 'Go to sleep, Harriet. You need it. But not for too long, my sexy little friend. The night has only just begun...'

CHAPTER EIGHT

'HARRIET! Wake up. Harriet! Do you realise it's past noon?'

Harriet turned over with a groan, clutching the duvet tightly around her. She didn't want to wake up, she wanted to stay asleep, dreaming all those wonderful erotic dreams. Why couldn't her mother just . . . ?

Her eyes shot open, blinking up into Julia's disapproving face. 'Mother?' Harriet squeaked, panicky eyes darting around the room before a sigh of relief fluttered from her lips. It wasn't Brad's bedroom. It was her own.

A half-incredulous smile softened her mouth as she remembered sneaking into the house shortly after five, tiptoeing along the hall like a naughty teenager.

'I wanted to speak to you, Harriet,' her mother said crisply, 'and I couldn't wait any longer. Oh, my goodness, look at your lovely suit just thrown down on the floor!' She bent to sweep up the skirt and jacket, shaking them irritably and hanging them over a chair. 'It's not like you, Harriet, to be so untidy.'

Harriet's face flushed guiltily as she recalled having come home wearing nothing but that suit. No bra. No pants. Nothing. She had discarded her clothes in the darkness and slipped into bed stark naked, her lips still pulsing with the feel of Brad's last lingering kiss. Sleep had come quickly, however, the deep sleep of a thoroughly contented and happy woman.

'You must have got in late last night,' her mother said half accusingly. 'I was still up at one-thirty and you hadn't come home.'

A rebellious surge stopped Harriet from hurrying to justify her actions. She was twenty-six years old, she reasoned. A grown woman, not a child. She stretched her still languorous body and sighed. 'I did get in fairly late,' she admitted nonchalantly. 'I went back to Brad's place for a drink after dinner and a mist rolled in. We waited till it cleared before coming home.'

'You mean to say you were alone with that man at his place till all hours of the night?' There was no doubting the shock-horror of the tone. And the 'that man' had an ominously disapproving note to it as well.

This rather surprised Harriet, given the circumstances. 'I would have thought that wouldn't bother you, Mother,' she said with increasing irritation, 'since you want me to marry Mr Barrington. I believe ladies of your generation often caught their men by deliberately getting pregnant.'

'Don't be rude, Harriet! I know full well you wouldn't do anything like that. But some men are——'

'Why wouldn't I?' Harriet cut in sharply.

Julia's eyes widened as Harriet lifted a hand to push her hair out of her eyes. The quilt had slipped, revealing naked shoulders. 'Harriet! You haven't got anything on!'

Harriet froze. She didn't really want her mother to know the lie of the land, so she adopted a convincingly innocent expression, yawning as she pulled the quilt back up. 'I couldn't find my nightie,' she said blithely. 'I was so tired I went to bed in my knickers.' She hoped her mother's eagle eyes didn't spy the bulging handbag in which her knickers still resided. 'What was it you wanted to talk to me about?'

Julia looked uncomfortable and began moving agitatedly around the room, fiddling with things. Harriet held her breath as she walked past and blessedly ignored the handbag lying on the dressing-table.

'It's about Mr Barrington,' Julia began tentatively.

'Mr Barrington?' Harriet repeated with raised eyebrows. 'What happened to Brad?'

Julia sniffed. 'I don't think I want you to be on such friendly terms with that man any more.'

'Good heavens, why not?'

She swung to face Harriet with troubled eyes. 'I picked up one of Mr Barrington's novels at the library yesterday and read some of it last night while you were out. I have to tell you, Harriet, I was shocked! Truly shocked! Why, it was...it was...disgusting! People doing all sorts of things to each other. Like animals! I mean...what sort of man writes books like that?'

Harriet resisted smiling. Brad's books weren't *that* bad! Sexy, yes. And explicit. But he steered well clear of anything obscene.

'A clever commercial writer, I would say, Mother,' she defended honestly. 'Remember, his books sell in the millions. People like them, ordinary people like you and me. They *are* very sexy, but not pornographic.'

'You *like* his books, Harriet?'

She shrugged. 'I didn't consider his first two very memorable, but, yes, I enjoyed them for what they were. This new one, though...' she leant over and picked up the copy of *High-Rise* from her bedside table '...now this book is a different kettle of fish entirely.'

Julia took it from her daughter's outstretched hand and made a face at the cover. 'Looks the same to me!'

'You know what they say,' Harriet laughed. 'Don't judge a book by its cover.'

'You mean there's no sex in it?'

'Of course there's sex in it, just as there's sex in life. You sleep with Father, don't you?'

'Harriet!'

'Oh, Mother, stop sounding like Queen Victoria. Not that she could talk, the sexy old thing. People like reading about relationships between people, and, on the whole, relationships involve sex.'

Julia gave her daughter a speculative look. 'And what kind of *relationship* are you having with our celebrity author?' she asked point-blank.

Harriet knew her mother would never understand the agreement Brad and she had come to during the night. 'We're just good friends,' she said without a flicker.

The disturbing thought came to Harriet that she might have lost more than her virginity last night. Her conscience seemed to have gone out of the window as well. But she quickly acknowledged with less self-reproach that she had a right to privacy, and a right to a private life. She was an adult woman, and, as such, did not have to answer to her parents. Not only that, she knew her mother would just worry about her if she knew the truth.

'And when will you be seeing each other again?' her mother asked, still suspicious.

Harriet adopted a carefree expression. 'Brad did say something about helping me with my play next Friday evening. He thinks it has potential. And Mrs Gallagher has invited us both to tea Saturday night,' she added, which led to her relaying the story of the kittens.

This was the right approach, Harriet quickly saw, her mother's fears being quickly soothed as Brad came over as no more than a kind-hearted neighbour. When Harriet expressed a wish to shower and dress, Julia left the room without further fuss.

Harriet threw the covers from her nakedness and sprang from the bed, dashing into the bathroom with a zest for life she had not felt for years. She snapped on the shower, testing the water till it was hot enough then stepping inside. The steaming jets beat down on her upturned face, her hands slicking her hair back, her eyes shutting to feel the invigorating heat of the water on her skin.

Her skin...

It prickled into goose-bumps as Harriet's mind flashed back to the early hours of that morning when Brad had gently awakened her with a kiss shortly after one. Without another word he had scooped her up and carried her into his old-fashioned bathroom, astonishing her by lowering her body into a tantalisingly scented bath, then proceeding to delicately wash her all over.

In retrospect she found it hard to believe she had accepted his personal ministrations without protest or embarrassment. It was as though he had cast a spell over her. Under his eyes and hands she felt truly beautiful, beautiful and desired. She had melted back into his arms after the bath, allowing him intimacies that might have ordinarily shocked her, but had, at that time, seemed so natural. He had pleasured her over and over before once again taking full possession of her body.

Afterwards, they had lain in each other's arms, talking, and she had asked him why he had come to live on their remote mountain, giving voice to the momentary fear she'd had the other day about his being ill.

He'd looked blank for a moment before she elaborated, whereupon he'd laughed drily.

'Sorry to disappoint you, Harriet, but I'm not dying of some rare disease. And my ticker is as strong as Big Ben. What an imagination you have! No, I bought this isolated retreat because I wanted somewhere quiet to live. I'm going to write a bigger, better book, Harriet. Something different from anything I have tried before, something with more scope and depth, an Australian saga, told from our early days right up to the present. I think that here…in these quiet hills…I might be able to find enough strength and solitude to attempt it.'

'Don't you think your readers might be disappointed?' she pointed out to him.

He grinned. 'No… There'll still be plenty of sex in it. Now, no more about me, Madam Prosecutor. Tell me about yourself. Why, for instance, is a woman of your intelligence hiding her light under a bushel in a small country school?'

'I've only come home to live this last year,' she told him. 'I taught in Sydney before.'

'Hmm. Strange… I would have thought a single woman like yourself would have stayed in Sydney where the eligible bachelors are. You're not really a rabid feminist, are you, Harriet? I mean, you *do* want a husband and family one day, don't you?'

She turned her face away then, afraid that her eyes would betray even more than her play had, but he would have none of it, turning her face back to his, kissing away her pain and encouraging her to tell him things she had never told another human being. It was difficult, though, to find words for her utter devastation at the time of Graham's default, almost impossible to describe her despair over what Amanda had done, and the subsequent total loss of what little confidence she had in herself as a woman.

The telling made it all flood back to her and she cried then, letting him hold her close and whisper soft, soothing words in her ear. And with his sweet

kindness her faith in human beings was partly re
stored. Brad might lead what some people woul
consider an unconventional, even an amoral life
she conceded. But he could be a gentle man,
compassionate man, who, Harriet felt confident
would never deliberately hurt her as Graham an
her sister had done.

She spoke more freely after the tears, telling hin
about the lonely months of her life after she'd bee
jilted.

'I thought I had pulled myself together,' sh
recalled with a dry laugh. 'I found a new flat, go
a new job at a Sydney high school and started going
out on the weekends, to the movies, the theatre.
was even asked out a couple of times on real dates
Or so I thought at the time. But the men who aske
me out, Brad... They pulled no punches. The
asked for sex straight out, straight away...' Sh
shook her head. 'They made no pretence at love
or even liking. One was quite nasty when I sai
no... Called me a stuck-up bitch with a ridicu
lously high opinion of myself.'

'Pig,' Brad agreed softly, and hugged her som
more.

Things had built up and up inside her, she tol
him, till one day last October she had started crying
in the staff room and hadn't been able to stop.
Unbeknown to her parents, a doctor from the
Department of Education had sent her to a rest
home for several weeks then advised a complete
change of scene, so she had come home to live an
teach in the country.

Brad said he understood how destroyed she must have felt over what her sister and Graham had done, and how her subsequent experiences with men could have soured her outlook.

'But people do need people, Harriet,' he advised. 'Men need women, and women need men.'

And he proceeded to show her, without words, that she particularly needed him.

On the drive home in the early hours of the morning Brad kept extolling his opinions of her and her future. 'Marriage is not necessary for a good sex life,' he said. 'And you're not plain, Harriet. Physically you're very attractive and will grow even more attractive as you grow older. Perhaps, in the past, young men have found your intelligence intimidating, even threatening. They have fragile egos which respond better to the more traditionally dependent female. But as they get older men look for different qualities from big boobs and batting eyelashes. How old was your Graham?'

'Twenty-four at the time of our engagement. He'd be twenty-eight now.'

'Hmm. From what you've told me he was probably drawn to you initially on a mental level, but he would not have asked you to marry him if he hadn't desired you physically as well. Something held him back. Perhaps he was sexually inexperienced, or lacked confidence in that area for some reason.'

'Do you think so?' Harriet murmured, not entirely convinced, sceptical that a man as dashing as Graham had been lacking in sexual confidence or experience.

Brad shrugged. 'I can't be sure but I think I have made a reasonable assumption. Either way, Graham is the past, Harriet. It's the future you must concern yourself with. One day soon you will forget all about Graham, fall in love and marry some lucky man. But in the meantime...'

'In the meantime?' she'd asked breathlessly.

'In the meantime, I'd like to be your lover,' he'd offered in conclusion.

In the meantime...

Harriet frowned now as she soaped up her stomach. At the time, fresh from the pleasure of his arms, she had not even considered refusing Brad's proposition. But now it all sounded depressingly temporary.

Yet she had known all along what sort of man he was. He had never hidden the way he chose to live his life. Women came and went. His only concession to normal moral standards was that there was only one at a time. And it seemed that for the time being he wanted the woman in his bed to be Harriet.

She could not deny that the prospect excited her. Brad was a wonderful lover, incredibly tender but amazingly imaginative. He said deliciously wicked things to her, did deliciously wicked things to her, yet all the while she felt surprisingly loved.

That brought her up with a jolt.

Don't go letting your own imagination run away with you, Harriet, she warned herself, and snapped off the water. Brad doesn't fall in love. He likes you, and by some miracle desires you. Leave it at that.

She stepped out of the shower, reached for a towel and began rubbing herself dry.

But what of your feelings for Brad?

Her hands stilled at the contraction of her heart. Wasn't she perhaps already forgetting Graham, already falling in love?

Harriet's romantic soul seemed to be demanding she must be. How else could she feel what she felt when Brad made love to her?

But then her logical mind took over. Brad had a way with women. That was the truth of the matter. She was suffering, not from the pangs of true love, but from a case of sexual infatuation after years of loneliness and frustration.

A sudden knocking on the bathroom door startled her.

'Harriet! Phone for you. It's Brad.'

Brad? Brad was phoning? The 'don't expect phone calls' Brad? He'd warned her that when he wrote he forgot everything, not just the time, so never made promises he might not keep. He had even suggested that she'd better drive herself over after school the following Friday rather than rely upon his picking her up.

'Coming,' she called back through the door. 'I'll take it in Dad's study.'

'Very well.' Her mother's footsteps sounded her retreat.

Harriet stumbled naked out into her bedroom, pulled on her dressing-gown and ran. Her father's study was only two doors along the hall and, it being a Saturday, was sure to be empty. She dashed into the rarely used room and snatched the receiver up from the desk. 'Brad? What's wrong? You said you wouldn't ring.'

'My, my, is that heavy breathing for me?'

She laughed. 'I was in the shower and didn't like to keep you waiting so I ran.'

'Don't tell me you're starkers!'

'I did put a robe on.'

She heard him suck in a deep breath then expel it slowly.

'What was it you wanted, Brad?' she asked shakily.

'I guess I was concerned about you,' he admitted in a brusque voice.

'Concerned?'

'Yes...' His hesitancy sent a prickling up her spine. 'Sometimes things feel very differently the morning after the night before. I thought I'd give you an out.'

'An out?'

'Don't be obtuse, Harriet. You know what I mean. You can call it quits now if you like. We could go back to being just friends. I won't pressure you.'

Harriet's whole chest tightened with a hurt dismay. Had last night meant so little to him that he could dismiss it so easily? She had thought they had at least established a special relationship, an intimacy that was based on caring and sharing as much as sex.

But then Harriet remembered she was hardly the sort of woman a man couldn't bear to part with. She had forgotten that for a short while. Brad had *made* her forget it, with his softly flattering words and seemingly sincere actions.

'Perhaps you're the one who wants an out,' she said sharply.

An electric silence fell on to the line.

Seconds stretched into a minute.

Panic set in that their affair might indeed be over, practically before it had begun. Harriet couldn't have borne that. Not yet.

'Brad?' she said in husky tones. 'Brad, are you still there?'

'Yes... I'm here.'

How odd he sounded. Sad. Weary.

'I'm sorry,' she said in an anguished voice. 'But I thought you wanted to call it off and were twisting it around to make it seem as though it was my idea...'

His sigh was deep. 'Silly Harriet.'

'Then everything is still all right? With us?'

He laughed, but it had nothing of his usual amused dryness in it. It was more... bitter. 'Yes, Harriet, for as long as your little body desires.'

'Don't you mean heart?' she joked, hoping to jolly him out of his strange mood. It wasn't like Brad to be down.

'I thought we agreed that hearts had nothing to do with our relationship,' he warned curtly.

So that was it, she realised. Brad was worried that she might fall for him. She could understand his concern—given his attitude to emotional involvement—since she herself had been on the borders of confusing sexual satisfaction with love.

'Come, now, Brad,' she retorted lightly. 'Even liking comes from the heart and you must know how much I like you. Don't you like me too?'

'Don't get coy, Harriet.'

'You're not worrying that I might fall in love with you, are you? I may be relatively naïve, but I'm not a masochist!'

Now his laughter sounded more normal and relaxed. 'I'm glad to hear that. Well, I suppose I should get back to the grindstone,' he drawled. 'Books don't write themselves, worse luck.'

'I thought you enjoyed writing.'

'I do...after I get going. But getting going can be a trial, particularly when I keep thinking about a certain lady.' He sighed. 'Hell, I can't even go into the bathroom without having these fantastic visions. There's this naked woman, you see, in my bath, and I'm soaping up her skin...'

Harriet was glad he couldn't see her flaming face at that moment.

'Now that I think of it, perhaps that certain lady might like to come over today,' he whispered huskily. 'I could put off my writing and we could——'

Her laughter cut him off, laughter that was more a self-protection than anything else. Her body had burst into flames at his seductive spiel, so much so that she had been forced to put on mental brakes before she disintegrated into mush. A hot, persuasive voice inside her own brain kept urging her to say yes, to run to him, but another voice quickly joined in, warning her with equal force to refuse, advising her not to let her new-found desires get out of hand. 'Sorry, Casanova, I have other plans for today,' she said with creditable coolness.

'Such as?' he exclaimed, sounding surprised that she would refuse him.

'I have thirty essays on Shakespeare to mark, not to mention a whole host of household chores. We ordinary folk don't have cleaners and cooks to come in and do our work for us,' she pointed out, reminding him of the daily he had hired to come in Monday to Friday.

'You're cruel, Harriet, do you know that?'

'I've had good teachers.'

'Surely you're not referring to me?' he mocked. 'I'm the original softie.'

'There's nothing soft about you, Brad Barrington.'

'For which women are eternally grateful!' he said wickedly.

She went red as a beetroot. 'You're disgusting.'

'Compliments, compliments. So...I have to wait till Friday, do I? Ah, well...be it on your head. I won't be responsible for how I'll be after six long days away from you.'

He hung up, leaving Harriet far too stirred up for her own peace of mind. She sashed the robe around her agitated nakedness and returned to her bedroom, where she threw herself down on to the rumpled sheets. She knew she should be appalled with herself for becoming mixed up with such a scandalous man, but somehow she couldn't dredge up either the energy or the motivation. All she could think of was that she wished she had given in to Brad's proposal.

She sighed and rolled over, staring blankly up at the ceiling. The coming week loomed ahead as very long and very dull.

It didn't turn out quite so bad after all. On the Sunday Pete Hollis, her dyslexic student, had some good news about the tinted spectacles she had recommended he try as a possible cure. His doctor had made enquiries and he was flying to Sydney the following day to have them fitted. His hopeful happiness had conveyed itself to Harriet, who genuinely liked the shy lad.

Then on Monday a couple of the teachers at school commented on how great she was looking. The librarian asked her if she had bought something special for her complexion, since it was so rosy. 'Or is it just the spring air?' the rather intuitive woman added.

Harriet had laughed away the comments but they had left her feeling ridiculously pleased, since compliments about her appearance were rare occurrences in her life. Lovemaking must agree with her, she decided.

Then on Tuesday one of the older boys in year ten whistled at her. She had smiled back at him, which brought another whistle from one of his mates. This all conspired to make Harriet feel like a new woman, so much so that on the Thursday evening she went shopping for some new clothes to befit her quickly growing self-confidence.

She invested in three skirts, all shorter and tighter than her usual tailored style, and a couple of pairs of softer, more femininely cut trousers. She matched them with tops that were far removed from the slightly masculine shirts she usually bought. While not skimpy or frilly, they were still feminine, made in soft, sensual materials and muted sexy hues. Oyster, pearl and dusky pink.

Her final purchase was a deceptively sexy black mohair jumper that had a plain front, but was slashed deep at the back. Only a couple of criss-cross woollen straps stopped the garment from falling right off her shoulders. She intended wearing it on Friday evening, teamed with the new khaki-coloured suede skirt that featured a daring slit up one side. Actually the skirt was so tight that if it hadn't had the slit she wouldn't have been able to walk at all.

Harriet went to bed after shopping feeling hopelessly excited, sleep coming with difficulty. When she awoke the next morning, the feeling of excitement had increased, if anything, bringing sick nerves to her stomach. In a few hours she would be with Brad, and, despite having told her mother he wanted to help her with her play, Harriet knew that was merely an excuse. What he wanted was to take her to bed again.

Occasionally during the week Harriet had found it hard to believe that the previous weekend had happened, that Brad actually desired her. Some ghastly inner voice kept telling her this situation couldn't last, that it was only a matter of time before Brad dumped her for someone else.

But this Friday morning another voice refused to think about such things any more. She determined to grasp what pleasure she could find in life one day at a time. And today was the day she would be back in Brad's arms.

She was distracted at school, feeling both relieved and nervous when the break-up bell finally rang. Her driving suffered on the way home, and she was grateful that her mother was out at one of her bridge afternoons. The last thing she wanted was some awkward questions about why she was having her second shower that day, or why she was wearing new sexy clothes just to work on her play.

The clothes were a dead giveaway, she realised, as she frowned at herself in the full-length mirror in Amanda's room. In fact, they shouted to anyone who saw her that here was a woman looking for male admiration, male desire, male attention. All of a sudden Harriet's confidence failed her. They looked too obvious, too...cheap?

'No... I can't wear these,' she breathed agitatedly. But as she whirled to leave the room she caught sight of a photograph of her sister on a shelf, one that showed a pouting confident mouth and deliberately provocative eyes.

'Oh, yes, I damned well can!' Harriet burst out, gritting her teeth and marching from the room.

CHAPTER NINE

BRAD must have heard Harriet drive up for he came to meet her, striding down the front steps, looking casually macho in a natty grey tracksuit and joggers. Harriet swallowed as her gaze swept up over him, once again hardly believing that this incredibly handsome man was her lover. A quiver of excitement rippled through her as he yanked open the door of her car.

His eyebrows lifted when his gaze landed on her smart clothes, particularly the slit in her skirt where a great proportion of stockingless thigh was on display. 'We're not going out, you know,' he said.

She was quite proud of the confident smile she presented as she swung her long legs sideways. 'I know that, but I felt like dressing up. What do you think?' she added, standing up and turning slowly around.

'Disgusting,' was his verdict.

Her face fell.

'But I love it.' He grinned wickedly, pulling her to him in an abrupt embrace. 'God, I've missed you, Harriet.'

His swift, savage kiss startled her, but she found her hands automatically snaking up around his neck so that they were even closer, chest to chest, stomach to stomach, thigh to thigh. It amazed her how quickly she had become addicted to Brad's body. She couldn't seem to get enough of him.

'No bra, Harriet?' he whispered thickly.

She swallowed, her mouth going dry as he moved his chest against her nipples.

'Did you want me to wear one?' she asked breathlessly.

'Hell, no! If you did I wouldn't be able to do this.' And his hands slid up under the black mohair to roam at will across her naked flesh before working their way under her arms and round to her bare nipples.

'Must you do that out here?' she gasped.

'Why not? We're alone.'

'You're making me dizzy.'

'Good,' he muttered thickly. And he kissed her again.

She broke her mouth away. 'I think we should go inside.'

'Uh-huh,' he negated.

'But——'

'I want to see the sky in your eyes when I make love to you.'

Harriet reeled with shock. Surely he didn't mean to take her out there in the open, under the setting sun? Surely not . . .

But when his mouth bent again, his tongue slipping between her lips as slowly and seductively as his hands were moving over her breasts, the momentary concern began to recede. She stared into his lazy, smoky eyes, any wish to object now totally lost within her own growing passion. She herself now wanted more than his tongue invading her.

More than his thumbs rubbing her nipples. *Much* more.

She groaned, desire and frustration mixing with a type of dismay. It wasn't right, she thought, to be so susceptible to this man's expertise. It gave him too much power. He would become like a drug that she had to have, no matter what the cost to her personal happiness and survival.

But all these arguments did not sway her increasingly aroused body. Her aching flesh forged ahead, with a will of its own, undulating against Brad's in a blatantly wanton display of desire. How it even *knew* how to act that way appalled what remained of Harriet's conscious mind. But know it it did, unerringly, tantalisingly, its effect on Brad quite staggering.

His eyes squeezed tightly shut and he groaned, a raw, naked growl that contradicted all she believed of him, that he was a cool lover, a man who, while finding pleasure in sex, was always in some measure of control.

But this was not a man in control, she quickly realised as his mouth turned unexpectedly wild on hers. She almost choked at the now unsparing assault of his tongue and when his hands left her breasts to grip her hips with bruising strength, panic gripped her. She even tried to pull away.

But there was no stopping him. He urged her backwards till she was hard up against the car, at the same time his hands surging down, then up her thighs, taking her skirt with him. For a brief moment the cool breeze chilled her heated flesh, but then all she felt was Brad's fingers stroking her through the thin silk of her bikini briefs.

Now her mouth burst from his, gasping for breath, though there was no longer any question of protest. Pure pleasure and need had worked their relentless seduction so that her world had shrunk to nothing more than Brad's caresses, and her own liquid throbbing response.

'I want you now, Harriet,' he rasped. 'For God's sake don't stop me.'

'I won't,' she gasped back.

She heard her pants rip, felt the shocking yet arousing sense of total exposure. And then she was helping him push aside his clothes, moving her body to facilitate his entry, arching her back and urging him on, her hands mad in his hair, her mouth desperate beneath his.

She gasped when he drove up into her, dimly aware that her back was hurting where the handle of the door was digging into it. But she was uncaring of the pain, uncaring of anything but satisfying the need to be as one flesh with Brad.

And he answered that need, his movements as fast and frantic as hers, filling her completely with his thrusting hardness, taking her swiftly to that point where everything hung for one last shatteringly suspended moment before diving headlong into ecstasy. She climaxed before he did, sagging into him as her legs went from under her. With a groan he swept her up and lowered her to the ground, where he continued till he too found release before slumping across her in shuddering exhaustion.

It was some time before either of them spoke.

And then it was Brad, his words carrying a disturbing self-disgust as he lifted himself from her and yanked down her grass-stained skirt. 'Hell, Harriet,' he groaned. 'I'm sorry...'

'It's...it's all right,' she said, but her voice was shaking. Reaction, she supposed, from the violence of their passion.

'I'm a bastard,' he muttered as he adjusted his clothes.

The desolation on his face made Harriet reach out and gently touch his face, his lips.

'Don't say that, Brad. I didn't mind. Why should I? I enjoyed it.'

He grabbed her hand, kissing her palm with astonishing feeling before letting it go. 'I know. That's what I mean. Hell, Harriet, don't you see? I'm taking your blossoming sexuality and using it for all it's worth. *Using* it! I'm not even offering you anything in return.'

Harriet's heart turned over at Brad's distress, although she wasn't sure why he was so upset. He had laid everything on the line from the word go. 'I'm not sure I understand, Brad,' she said agitatedly. 'If you're using me, aren't I using you just as much?'

He glared at her, his eyes truly pained.

'You said we were friends,' she went on, afraid now, afraid he was leading up to something she might not want to hear. 'Friends don't use each other. Friends help each other. Can't you see how much you have helped me, Brad? I'm already a dif-

ferent woman, a happier, more confident one. I'll
be eternally grateful to you.'

He sighed. 'I hope so, Harriet. I honestly couldn't
live with myself if I felt I was going to somehow
hurt you. You must know how different you are
from my normal choice of woman. You're softer,
kinder, more vulnerable——'

'Not that vulnerable. I've been through hell,
Brad, because of a man. I won't be sent back there
easily.'

He gave her a long, considering look before
taking her hand and helping her to her feet. Her
legs were still like jelly and when she leant weakly
against him he scooped her up in his arms.

He was carrying her up the steps when Harriet
suddenly went dead white. 'Oh, my God,' she
gasped.

He stopped dead in his tracks. 'What? What's
wrong?'

'I... You...just now...you didn't use anything—and it's right in the middle of my cycle.'

Brad sighed and moved on, carrying her in grim
silence up the steps and inside before placing her
in one of the lounge chairs. 'I'll run you a bath,'
he said, and walked away without another word.

A bath? A bath was no means of contraception!
Harriet's dazed mind raced back to the other night.
Had he used something then? She didn't really
know. The bedroom had been fairly dark. He had
turned away from her occasionally and to be
truthful she hadn't been concentrating on such
matters. After his initial reassurance, such matters
had slipped her mind. She had just assumed.

Just assumed...

A wave of dismay crashed through her. Surely Brad wasn't the sort of man who took mad chances, and then, when caught, insisted on an abortion? Didn't he know she would never have an abortion? She couldn't do that to a baby, her baby, Brad's baby.

Brad's baby...

A mental picture shot into her mind of herself, having Brad's baby. It was far from an appalling picture. After the initial shock it was surprisingly warm and wonderful.

A quiet joy began to grow in her heart as the dream ran wild, even to Brad's gradually coming to care for the child, and, through it, her. True, total joy. And when he walked back into the room Harriet's heart jolted with a sudden new awareness.

I love him, she realised. And it took her breath away.

'Yes?' he demanded, seeing her face change.

Harriet could not find her voice, so weak did she feel at her discovery. But soon after the weakness came certainty. Yes, it was a different love from what she had felt for Graham. Very different. This was far more real. It was deep and earthy and physical, not airy-fairy and make-believe. If anything, Graham had been the infatuation, not Brad.

A determination such as Harriet had never felt before swept through her. She would secure this man's love if it was the last thing she ever did. Maybe he would never give up his bachelor lifestyle and marry her, but that was not the only alternative. Caring and commitment could be expressed in lots of ways.

'Brad,' she began carefully. 'I want to tell you not to worry, that if there is a baby——'

'There won't be any baby,' he cut in flatly.

'But . . . but I was right, wasn't I? You didn't use any contraceptive . . .'

He walked over to stand at the fireplace, picking up a poker to strike idly at the dead ash in the hearth. 'You're absolutely correct,' he said at last, lifting shockingly hard eyes. 'I didn't use anything. I don't need to. I've had a vasectomy.'

She could only stare at him, his words striking at her very soul like a death-knell.

'A vasectomy,' she repeated in a hollow voice.

'You don't have to look so appalled,' he went on coldly. 'It was a decision I made years ago and to be frank, it's worked out surprisingly conveniently in more ways than one.'

She frowned, struggling to put aside her ghastly wretchedness to work out what he was saying. 'But why, Brad?' she asked. 'What made you make such a decision? Don't tell me you did it so that you could sleep around without consequences, because I won't believe you.'

Her fierce assertion that he would not be so callous did not find any favour with him. If anything, his face grew stonier. 'More fool you,' he growled. 'But you're right, that wasn't my initial reason. Though what does it matter what my reason was, now . . . ?'

He clammed right up, leaving Harriet feeling totally frustrated. She had to know what had happened. She just had to!

'I... I've told you about my past, Brad,' she prompted gently. 'Don't you think I deserve the same confidences? Isn't that what friendship is all about? It was you who said people need people. Talk to me, Brad. Tell me about it.'

He glared at her for a moment, than a sardonic smile creased back his grim mouth. 'To think I would have my own words turned against me...'

She smiled at him, a warm, encouraging smile.

But his eyes grew hard again. Harriet's heart sank even further.

He saw her shoulders sag and shrugged. 'Very well, but don't go thinking I'm some tragic figure, Harriet. I can't abide pity and, as I said, it turned out to be a very fortuitous decision.'

He hesitated then, but she refused to say a word, to give him any further excuse not to get on with his explanation.

His sigh was irritable. 'I had a vasectomy to protect my wife...'

She controlled her shock well, her only betraying gesture a slight stiffening of her spine.

'I was very young when I married Helen. Only twenty-one, fresh from university with an arts degree in literature and a burning desire to write. Helen agreed to support me so that I could write full-time. We were idealistic, you see, thinking that love and sacrifice and hard work would win out in the end.'

His laugh sounded very bitter.

'But of course life isn't quite so simple. Seven years later I had five rejected manuscripts in a drawer and a pregnant wife. The pill, you see, can be remarkably unreliable for a person who is frequently on antibiotics for one infection or another, and Helen was proving to have increasing health problems. Without going into medical details, her pregnancy had complications. She miscarried in her fifth month and almost died. Her doctor advised that another baby could be fatal. I chose a vasectomy because I thought Helen had suffered enough. As fate would have it she fell ill with a virus only months afterwards. It lodged in her heart and she died. That's it. That's the story.'

He looked up at Harriet, shocking her with his hardness. There was not a glimmer of emotion, not a trace of distress. It was as though he had taken that chapter in his life and coated its memory with some inpenetrable substance. And, while she felt a deep sympathy for what he had gone through, what Harriet could not condone was the way he had chosen to live his life since then. My God, his wife had died nearly a decade ago! And, while it was tragic that he couldn't father children, there was still a lot a man like Brad could give to a relationship. There was no need for him to go from woman to woman, spurning love and commitment. It was not only wrong, but a cruel waste!

The more she thought about it the more she felt frustrated, rather than sympathetic. There he was telling *her* to face up to things when he had obviously chosen the easy way out himself, running away from just about everything! And how dared he call his vasectomy fortuitous? It showed just how far his self-delusion went. For self-delusion it was, Harriet was sure. The flashes of true kindness and compassion she had seen in Brad did not jell with this callous brute he resorted to being whenever anyone or anything got too close to him. Maybe he was afraid of being hurt again. Most likely he was. But that was no excuse, not after this length of time! Harriet resolved to break through that brittle façade if it was the last thing she did.

'I see,' she said, a steely determination welling up inside her.

'Do you? I wonder.'

'Of course I do.' There was an edge to her voice that attracted his attention. 'After the tragedy of your wife's death you became bitter. You had done your best, you thought, with your writing and your family. All to no avail. So you started writing pacy though trashy novels, in a type of revenge at life, spurning the ideals you had once held so dear. Were you shocked, Brad, at your success? Or were you even more bitter? And then there were your women, of course. Flashy, empty women who could satisfy your male needs but nothing else. For what else was there to satisfy? Nothing... Because you're an empty shell of a man, Brad. A useless, empty shell of a man...'

She saw his face go red, saw his fury expand inside him till it was bursting at the seams. She welcomed his angry march across the room, welcomed his bruising hands wrenching her out of the chair. For she had got through to him, cruelly maybe, and with possibly unjust exaggeration of his behaviour. But it was working, peeling away that rock-like layer to uncover the real man below.

'God damn you, Harriet,' he fumed. 'God damn you!'

And then he kissed her, wildly, madly, ravaging her mouth and pulling her down to the floor.

'That's right,' she goaded him when she could tear her mouth free. 'Take all your frustrations out through sex. That's the only way you know how to express feelings any more, isn't it, Brad? You can't even be properly angry like anyone else.'

For a split second she was certain he was going to hit her. But he didn't, holding himself stiffly away as he gradually got himself under control. 'I think you'd better go home, Harriet,' he ground out, 'before things get totally out of hand here.' He levered himself up on to his feet and turned his back on her.

'No!' she said, and scrambled upright.

He whirled around, his face livid. 'God, don't you ever do as you're told?'

'Not any more.'

'Not any more,' he muttered. 'Hell, what have I let loose on this world?'

'The real Harriet Weatherspoon.'

For a long time he glared at her, his barely controlled anger bringing a prickle of apprehension to Harriet. Perhaps she was getting out of her depth here, came the niggling doubt. Perhaps she had gone too far. Maybe she hadn't succeeded in reaching the real man at all. Maybe what she was seeing was just another side to his bitterness, a seething, violent side that wanted to strike out at life and everyone in it.

She watched, dry-mouthed, as that left eyebrow of his arched sardonically. 'So you're staying, are you?'

Instinct told her she should turn and run, but love tended to win over most things, even physical fear. She had to stay, had to try to make him see the error of his ways. Oh, she wasn't deluding herself any longer that she could make him love her. That was a pipe-dream. But she suspected he felt more for her than he had felt for any woman in a long time. He genuinely liked her. Of that she was sure.

'You don't know what you're doing,' Brad said brusquely.

Her chin lifted in a defiant, stubborn gesture. 'Yes, I do, I'm staying.'

His eyes narrowed and for a long moment he merely stared at her, his face as fixed as granite. Then suddenly he shrugged, resuming an expression he had clearly mastered. Offhand. Indifferent. 'Then you'd better have your bath, don't you think? The water will be getting cold. Meanwhile, I'll prepare us some supper.'

'All right.'

'Then later we have to talk.'

She swallowed. 'Talk? What about?'

'Us . . .'

''What about us?''

His glance was quite ruthless. 'This weekend is going to be our swan-song, Harriet. You're not cut out for this type of relationship. You're far too emotional. It was stupid of me to let things develop as they have.'

Harriet couldn't speak, her heart racing with a frantic desperation. But she had to speak, had to convince Brad she was capable of carrying on an affair or she would hardly ever see him again. The prospect was like a knife in her chest, ripping and tearing right into her soul.

Her light chuckle brought a swift frown to his forehead. 'Really, Brad, don't be so melodramatic! Of course I was emotional a moment ago... I was angry at you. And why not? You picked my past clean but told me nothing about yourself. You claimed to be my friend but you didn't trust *me*.' She moved slowly towards him. 'I like being with you. I like your making love to me. Don't send me away...'

She moved right up to him and placed her hands on his chest, sliding them up till they wound around his neck. She felt him tense up beneath her touch, and took encouragement from it. 'You said you liked sex, Brad,' she husked. 'Needed sex. You won't find another woman so easily here in Valley's End. Don't cut off your nose to spite your face...'

He looked deep into her eyes, as though trying to see what lay behind her surprisingly sophisticated offer. 'You should run for politics, Harriet,' he drawled at last. 'You have a way of putting forward the pluses very attractively, while ignoring the negatives. You do realise that you are wasting your time with me, don't you? You could be out there looking for Mr Right.'

'I will, Brad. Eventually. But in the meantime...'
An ironic smile came to her lips.

He smiled back, a cynical twist flavouring its
formation. 'You have a habit of doing that, don't
you—throwing my own words back into my teeth?'

'Now, Brad,' she murmured, reaching up on
tiptoe. 'Why don't you give that mouth of yours a
rest? You'll be needing it later on.'

She flinched when his hands swept up to grab her
wrists, pulling them down to her sides. He clasped
her face then in a steely grasp, taking her mouth
briefly and brutally before releasing it.

'These are adult games you're playing, Harriet,'
he warned in an ominous tone. 'I hope you never
forget the rules...'

CHAPTER TEN

'I'M SO glad you came, Harriet,' Mrs Gallagher said, then gave a sheepish laugh. 'I was rather afraid you might ring up and cancel.'

She and Harriet were alone in the kitchen, busily washing up after a most delicious baked lamb dinner.

'We wouldn't have missed it for the world.' Harriet smiled, thinking privately that she had been equally worried that Saturday morning. She had half expected Brad to ring all day and say he couldn't make it.

'You know, you're looking quite lovely these days, Harriet,' the old lady went on. 'Rosy-cheeked and bright-eyed.'

'I think the country air agrees with me,' Harriet said, looking down at the plate she was drying, and not into those incisive blue eyes.

'Are you sure it hasn't got something to do with that handsome young man in there? If I didn't know better I would have thought I was looking at true love.'

Harriet flushed guiltily. She was about to change the subject when she looked up to see Brad in the doorway watching her. 'Brad! You startled me.'

His expression revealed nothing. 'Did I?'

'You're taking the little kittie home tonight, aren't you, Brad?' Mrs Gallagher said, pulling the plug from the sink.

'Yes,' he replied and walked over to pick the still tiny animal up from the basket. 'Speaking of home, I'm afraid we'll have to be going, Harriet. I had a very late night last night,' he added to his hostess.

Harriet flushed a dark red, thinking of the wild, passionate night she had spent in Brad's arms. He had been insatiable, showing her ways of making love that she had only ever read about, his demands exhausting but immensely satisfying. She had driven herself home shortly before dawn, her body at peace but her mind in turmoil.

What was to become of her, tangling her life up with such a man? He had refused to discuss his past with her again, making it clear the subject was *verboten*. All he wanted from her, he said, was a willing body, and if she didn't like the arrangement then she knew what she could do. Pride should have made her throw his cold-blooded arrangement back in his face but she just couldn't. Love didn't have much pride.

'Thank you so much for coming,' Mrs Gallagher said as she accompanied them both to the front door. 'And thanks again for the typewriter, Brad. I haven't started typing my book yet but I will, I surely will.'

Harriet nursed Brigit while Brad drove, but, despite it only being ten o'clock, he didn't head for Mist Mountain as she had expected, turning instead in the direction of her own home. She sat in stunned silence after he pulled up under the trees that lined her lane. The moonlight was totally blocked out and the car seemed draped in a deathly darkness. A feeling of impending doom settled on Harriet.

'This is it, isn't it?' she said at last in a choked voice. When he didn't answer she whirled to face him, her hand trembling as she clutched the sleeping kitten in her lap. 'Why, Brad? *Why?*'

The kitten woke, and whimpered. Brad reached out and took it from her. Harriet couldn't make out his features in the blackness but she knew exactly what his expression would be. He'd perfected his hardness much better than she ever had.

'You heard what Mrs Gallagher said, didn't you?' she accused hotly. 'You think I'm in love with you.'

'Please don't make a scene, Harriet,' he said in a surprisingly strained voice.

Her laughter was bordering on hysterical. 'Me? Make a scene? I wouldn't be bothered. You're not worth the effort, Brad Barrington. How you could think that any self-respecting woman would fall in love with you is beyond me. You're an unfeeling bastard with nothing going for you but a virile body and a fertile imagination.'

'Harriet, I——'

'Oh, do shut up, Brad. You've said quite enough.' And with that she got out of the car and slammed the door. 'Don't call us,' she shouted through the window. 'We'll call you.' Then she spun on her heel and stalked off, tears stinging her eyes as she went.

It took several seconds for her to march across the road and up the front path, several seconds in which there was dead silence behind her. Why didn't he just drive off? she agonised. Go, and leave her to her misery!

Her hand was fumbling with her key when the engine finally roared into life, the sound striking a crippling blow to her heart. A sob caught in her throat as he roared up the street.

She rattled the key into the lock, at the same time trying to dash the tears from her eyes. Lights were still on inside and the last thing she wanted was to have her crying spotted.

Gathering herself, she opened the door and went in, only to find the lounge-room and kitchen well lit but blessedly empty. She snapped off the lights and hurried down to her bedroom, relieved that she would miss the inevitable inquisition at her relatively early return.

She was surprised to see her own light on under the door, and opened it with a degree of puzzlement.

'Hello, Harriet,' Amanda said from where she was lying on Harriet's bed in a dressing-gown, reading *High-Rise*.

'Good lord, what are *you* doing here?' Harriet said with grim dismay.

Amanda put down the book and levered herself up into a sitting position, pushing her long blonde hair out of her big blue eyes. 'My, my, such happiness at my return.'

Harriet gave her a dry look. 'You wouldn't expect me to be thrilled, would you?'

Amanda sniffed. 'I see you haven't lost that sharp tongue of yours, sister dear.' Those deceptively ingenuous blue eyes swept over Harriet from top to toe, narrowing as they went. 'But there have been some changes, haven't there? Quite the elegant sophisticate now, aren't we?'

Amanda snapped *High-Rise* shut and pointed to the back cover which sported a good photograph of Brad. 'So tell me, Harriet, is he as good a lover as he looks? Mummy told me all about him so don't bother denying it. A man like this wouldn't settle for the lukewarm platonic friendship you've been feeding to her.'

'Why should I deny anything to you?' Harriet retorted, finding a small measure of satisfaction in Amanda's look of surprise. 'Of course Brad and I are sleeping together. And since you asked, yes, he's a very good lover. The best.'

'Not that *you'd* have any means of comparison,' her sister shot back nastily.

Harriet managed to keep her cool, even to raising a sardonic eyebrow. 'You think so? Heavens, Amanda, you've been gone four years, three of which I spent in the big, bad city. You don't honestly think I spent all that time pining after poor dear Graham, do you?'

Amanda was left with her mouth open.

'Now would you mind getting off my bed?' Harriet demanded. 'I'm rather tired. I've been having some late nights lately,' she finished pointedly, leaving the other girl in no doubt what she was referring to.

Amanda made a face and stood up grudgingly, and for the first time Harriet noticed that she had put on a considerable amount of weight. The once-prized high breasts were too full now, and drooping, with years of going braless. Another close glance showed a puffiness to the face that wasn't at all flattering.

Harriet felt a weird sense of justice that her much-envied sister was past her prime at the ripe old age of twenty-three.

'You haven't asked me why I've come home,' Amanda said sulkily.

Harriet didn't look up from where she was tidying her bed. 'It was the first thing I said when I came in, Amanda,' she reminded her sister, 'but it didn't suit you to tell me then.'

'Oh, don't be such a smarty-pants, Harriet. God, you haven't changed at all, have you? Still lording your so-called intelligence over me, making me feel bloody inferior!'

Startled, Harriet straightened up and looked at Amanda. Really looked at her. Good heavens, she realised. She's jealous. She's always been jealous, of *me*!

Harriet was truly taken aback by her discovery. Amanda... jealous of *her*! Amanda... feeling the same sort of feelings *she* had felt, only for a different reason.

Any vengeful thoughts Harriet had been harbouring faded in the face of this amazing realisation, for if there was one thing she understood well it was the crippling effect of feeling in some way inferior to other human beings.

'I'm sorry, Amanda,' she said with genuine sincerity. 'I never realised. Look, sit down and tell me what's wrong. There is something wrong, isn't there?'

Amanda's face crumpled as she burst into tears. Without thinking Harriet raced around and drew her sister into a fierce hug, astonishing herself at the rush of pity and affection she was feeling for the girl in her arms. But hadn't she known, underneath, that she had always loved her sister? Wasn't that why her betrayal had hurt so much?

'Hush, there, Amanda,' she crooned softly. 'Don't cry. Harriet's here—I'll help you. Come along and sit down on the bed and tell me what's wrong.'

'You...you won't care,' the girl sobbed. 'You think I just took Graham off you to spite you, and I suppose I did, at first. But it wasn't all my fault. It really wasn't.'

She pulled back and looked up at Harriet, her eyes shimmering. 'All my life...I've felt so *stupid* compared to you. I never won any prizes at school. Not one! I was a nothing, just pretty, empty-headed little Amanda. Which wasn't fair!' she cried. 'I...I'm quite bright really, but no one ever saw that. So I decided if they thought I was a dumb blonde I'd be a dumb blonde. It felt good, too, having the boys all running after me and never you. But...but...'

Her expression mirrored true pain. 'They only wanted one thing, and they always dropped me in the end. And then you came home with Graham and he was everything I had always wanted, and he was with *you*! I felt sick with envy, do you hear? Sick! I...I did everything I could to take Graham off you. I admit it. He'd only had one woman before, you see, and he was nervous. She had ridiculed his performance so he'd been afraid to try again. But I made it easy for him, so very, very easy. I'm not sure if he fell in love with me or the sex, but I didn't care which because by then . . .' her tear-stained face twisted into a grimace of self pity and remorse '. . . by then, Harriet, oh, please forgive me, but I was deeply in love with Graham and I didn't know what to do except run away with him. He . . . he didn't want to. He wanted to face you, but I . . . I couldn't. I know you must hate me. I'd probably hate you if you did what I did, but I wish you didn't, Harriet. I can't bear being hated,' she wailed, slumping down on the bed and burying her face in her hands.

Harriet sat down next to her, a comforting hand on her shoulder. 'I don't hate you, Amanda. You're my sister and I love you.'

Amanda raised wide, blinking eyes. 'You do?'

Harriet smiled. 'Of course I do, you silly ninny.'

'Oh, Harriet!' Amanda cried, and threw her arms around her sister.

'Now, now, love, don't cry,' Harriet said sensibly, but finding the task of controlling her own tears a real battle. 'We have to stop this silly weeping. Come on, now, wipe your eyes and tell me what's wrong. I suppose it's something to do with Graham?' she prompted gently. 'He hasn't left you, has he?'

'No.' Amanda bit her bottom lip. 'I . . . I've left him.'

Harriet was astonished. 'But why?'

Amanda looked as if she was going to cry again. 'He . . . he's been unfaithful to me!' she burst out.

Harriet blinked her surprise, which in itself was surprising. He had jilted *her*, hadn't he, by running off with Amanda?

'Some trampy little student seduced him,' Amanda volunteered, any further tears drowned by anger. 'She spun him some yarn—you know he's the top lecturer in literature at the California institute now—about needing extra help. He started staying back to tutor her at night. Their affair was all over the campus in no time but of course I was the last to know. I confronted him with it and he didn't deny it. Oh, he was sorry enough, said he hadn't gone looking for it but since I hadn't been sleeping with him he——'

'Why weren't you sleeping with him?' Harriet cut in.

Amanda looked flustered. 'I...I hadn't been well...he didn't understand... What I mean is I couldn't tell him...I wasn't sure what to do——'

'For heaven's sake, Amanda,' Harriet interrupted frustratedly, 'get to the point!'

'You don't have to yell! The fact of the matter is...well, I'm pregnant and Graham doesn't know because I wasn't sure I wanted to be at first. I felt sick all the time but I thought...and now I'm getting fat and ugly and I just hate myself!'

'Pregnant...' Harriet closed her eyes. Pregnant, with Graham's child, and not sure if she wanted it. Whereas *she*...she would *never* have Brad's child. Oh, how unfair life was.

Harriet opened her eyes at last, stood up and walked across to pick up her hairbrush. Her fingers shook as she began to brush her hair.

'Well, Harriet? Help me!'

Harriet stopped brushing, her hand dropping wearily to her side. 'I can only advise you, Amanda. If you love Graham, really love him, then go back to him, tell him you forgive him then tell him you're going to have his child. I'm sure he'll marry you.'

'But I'm not sure I want to have a baby just yet,' Amanda muttered unhappily. 'Graham always said the thing he liked most about me was my figure. I ... I thought of having an abortion but in the end I ... I just couldn't. Do you think I did the right thing?'

Harriet turned on her sister with a sigh. 'Good heavens, Amanda, of course you did. How you could even consider aborting Graham's child in the first place is beyond me, anyway. You say you love him. Well, if you do, then you should have stayed and worked things out with him. You can't always run away from your problems, you know. You have to face them.' Now where have I heard that before? Harriet thought wryly.

'I know ...'

Amanda looked so down that Harriet walked over to give her another quick hug. 'Now, don't worry. You can telephone Graham and tell him.'

'No, no, I don't want to talk to him! I ... I said some stupid things. He ... he won't talk to me. I'll write perhaps. Yes, that's the best idea. I'll write.'

Harriet shook her head in exasperation. 'What stupid things?'

Amanda looked decidedly guilty. 'I ... I got so mad that I told him I'd been unfaithful too. He ... he might not believe the child is his.'

'And is it?'

'Harriet!'

'Is it?' the question was echoed without mercy.

'Yes, of course,' Amanda croaked. 'I've never been with another man since I met Graham. I love him. I really do…' The tears came again then. Real tears this time.

'Oh, Amanda,' Harriet sighed. 'Whatever have you done?'

Sunday was a dreadful day, once the news was out. All morning Amanda cried and Julia fretted, Raymond having retreated to his study in grim silence. Harriet, who had her own miseries to contend with, was not much better. Lunch was a silent, strained affair, after which Raymond slammed out to go to his office.

'To regain my sanity!' he pronounced.

The afternoon stretched before Harriet like a long road without a turning. She couldn't even look forward to her reading session with Pete Hollis since he no longer needed special lessons, his new coloured glasses having been a great success.

When the doorbell rang shortly after three-thirty Harriet went to answer it quite eagerly, hoping that a visitor might give the rest of the family motivation to pull themselves together at least for a little while. The last person Harriet expected to see on their doorstep was Brad.

'Oh!' she exclaimed in shock.

He was casually dressed in blue jeans and white wind-cheater, his long brown hair in disarray from the stiff breeze that was blowing. He still looked far too handsome, far too sexy.

'I came to return your play,' he said curtly.

Harriet knew she was staring at him, but she couldn't help herself. It was as though she couldn't bear to let this extra chance to look at him go by, as though she wanted to imprint on her mind a better memory than that last angry farewell. She noticed the slight stubble on his chin and realised he had gone back to his idea of growing a beard. It was an oddly depressing thought, as though he was wiping out any effect she might have had on his life.

'Your play, Harriet,' he repeated, and pressed it into her hands.

'Who is it, dear?'

Julia came to the door to check on their visitor. 'Oh, it's you, Brad,' she said brightly enough. Harriet realised she had done a good job of settling her mother's doubts about the man. 'Would you like to come inside for a while? I was just going to make a cup of tea.' Her mother was always hospitable and, after all, knew nothing of their true relationship, and subsequent break-up.

Brad looked hesitant, giving Harriet a worried glance. Her returning smile was filled with self-irony, for she knew that despite all that had happened, despite what being with him would do to her, she wanted to invite him in. 'Please, Brad,' she said.

There was no denying she had thrown him for six with her smile for he frowned at her before stepping inside. 'I can't stay long,' he said darkly.

Julia went on ahead to the kitchen while Brad lingered with Harriet in the foyer. 'Long enough to meet my sister, surely,' she said with amazing composure. 'Amanda's come home from America to stay for a while.'

His eyes opened wide, his expression telling her that he found her calm acceptance of her sister's return quite astonishing.

When she went to move off he grabbed her arm. 'Harriet, I——'

Amanda swept into the foyer, her sudden appearance cutting Brad off mid-sentence. 'Mummy says we have a visitor. Why, goodness me if it isn't the famous Brad Barrington. I've just been reading your lovely book. Harriet, you sly old thing, are you hiding this gorgeous man out here on purpose?'

She came forward, all smiles and coyness, sliding her arm around Brad's elbow as though that was where it had always been meant to be. 'I'm Amanda, by the way. Harriet's sister. Has she told you about me? I'll bet she hasn't.' A gay laugh fluttered from her throat as she led him off down the steps into the lounge-room. The last thing Harriet saw was Brad giving her a furiously desperate glance over his shoulder.

She almost laughed. Amanda's dramatic entrance and contrived exit seemed quite ridiculous through more mature eyes. Of course she wasn't seriously trying to take a man away from her older sister this time, Harriet recognised. Amanda just couldn't help falling into her usual pattern of flirtatious behaviour. She had been doing it so long she didn't know any other way of meeting a man.

Not once during the whole afternoon tea did Harriet feel worried that Brad might be attracted to Amanda. Not once, despite her sister trying every female trick in the book to bewitch their guest, from outright flattery to the usual gushing enquiries. Which was astonishing, given the circumstances. If ever Brad might be susceptible to another woman's advances, it was now. Though it was clear, right from the start, that he was not in the mood to be charmed. He was silent and aloof, giving only the briefest answers to Amanda's repeated questions. He also refused to be manipulated into sitting next to her on the chesterfield, choosing instead one of the armchairs.

'I just don't know how writers think up all those stories?' Amanda asked breathlessly as her mother carried the finished tea-tray back to the kitchen.

'I have a fertile imagination,' was his dry reply.

Harriet's eyes flew to him, thinking he might be mocking her, but his face was expressionless. He stood up abruptly, making some excuse about having to get back to his writing.

Harriet stood up also. 'How's Brigit settling in?' she asked before he could flee.

'Brigit? Who's Brigit?' Amanda sniffed, clearly put out that her usual charisma had failed abysmally.

'A nuisance,' Brad snapped without elaboration. He was having trouble hiding his dislike of Amanda, Harriet realised.

'Brad's new kitten,' she offered gently, bringing another swift frown from Brad. 'We found an orphan litter under his house. Mrs Gallagher's been looking after them. There are still three left. Would you like one?'

Amanda wrinkled her nose in distaste. 'Ugh, no! Pets are work. Besides, I'll be going back to America soon, won't I?'

'I suppose so. Come on, Brad, I'll show you to the door.'

He walked away with only the curtest goodbye to Amanda, his mouth set grimly. But he burst out at the door. 'How can you bear to be so nice to that bitch?' he flung at Harriet. 'My God, I'd like to kill her for what she did to you! Her and that other bastard!'

'Graham's not a bastard,' Harriet defended.

Brad rocked back on his feet. 'Harriet! You're *not* still in love with him, are you?'

Her heart turned over with a thud. What to say?

No, Brad, it's you I love?

If she did he would still go away, but feeling guilty, thinking she was hurt and miserable.

Yes, Brad, I still love him?

Would that make him feel safe? Would that bring him back to her? For how long? She couldn't hide her love for him indefinitely.

'I don't know, Brad,' she lied. 'I really don't know.' Then she added more truthfully, 'I think I will always hold an affection for Graham in my heart...'

Brad looked at her for a long time. 'You're an incredible woman, Harriet. Incredible. Believe me when I say I'm glad to have had you for a friend. I'm only sorry I didn't have the sense to leave it that way. But I didn't come here today to hold a post-mortem on my failings. I wanted to give you back your play, and to tell you I'm returning to the city to live.'

A black pit yawned under her already tottering heart. 'You're... you're selling Mist Mountain?' she said with true anguish. It was one thing having to abandon any hope of a real relationship between them. Quite another never to see him again.

'No... I'll keep it as an investment, but I can see I was wrong to come here. Sydney suits me better.'

'But... but what about your new book?'

His smile was cynical. 'I think I'll go back to writing what I know best. And what sells.' He stretched out his hand. 'Goodbye.'

Her hand trembled as she lifted it to meet his but he clasped it tightly, folding his other hand around it and giving it a gentle shake.

'And Harriet... put the play in a drawer somewhere. Get on with writing something new, something fresh, something from the future instead of the past. Use your imagination.' His smile was wry. 'You have one too, you know.'

When he dropped her hand she felt that her soul had been wrenched from her body. She watched him walk away, desperate to call him back, to say anything that would make him change his mind.

But she could think of nothing; and he kept on walking.

She closed the door with a ragged sigh, not wanting to watch him drive away for the last time.

CHAPTER ELEVEN

HARRIET was eternally grateful that the followin
day was a public holiday, and she didn't have to g
to school. She had slept poorly, and awoke feelin
under the weather, certainly not in the mood fo
teaching her lively but sometimes wearing student

The house was soon blessedly empty, with he
father going off to sell more property, and he
mother having persuaded Amanda to be taken o
a shopping excursion over at Coff's Harbou
where some of the shops would be open, despit
the holiday. Now over the shock, the soon-to-b
grandmother was beginning to make clucking noise
which could only be satisfied with baby purchase

Not that Harriet blamed her. Her mother, sh
knew, had always wanted a grandchild to spoil an
fuss over. As for her father... while not given t
displays of emotion, he had seemed to accept th
inevitable quite amicably by the time the previou
day had drawn to a close.

Harriet went back to bed after breakfast, dozin
fitfully till midday when she dragged herself ou
still feeling like death warmed up, but knowing tha
if she stayed in bed any longer she would get
fearful headache. A long hot shower, she decide
might revive her body, if not her spirits. She turne
on the hot water and climbed in, knowing tha

nothing could soothe her tortured heart and mind. They were chock-full of Brad and her futile love for him. And soon there was more than shower water running down her cheeks.

It was a bleak though composed Harriet who finally emerged from the bathroom. She pulled on a pair of stone-washed jeans and an old blue jumper which she thought matched her mood. But when she began brushing her hair at the dressing-table mirror her reflection told her she looked surprisingly sexy. The skintight trousers showed her long legs and trim bottom to advantage, and there was no hiding the way her firm breasts were outlined by the soft thin wool.

All in all she looked like a woman who had just come from her lover's bed—all flushed and still stirred.

Harriet stared at herself for several seconds in total astonishment. Did all women change after they'd experienced physical love? she wondered. Did they all look more provocative, more sensual? She didn't really know. All she knew was that this woman staring back at her was not the woman of a couple of weeks ago. This woman, despite her misery, despite her despair, was more vibrant and alive-looking than she had ever been. And it was all due to Brad. She would never forget him, never forget what he had done for her. Never... Even now, with everything seemingly futile, a slender thread of hope remained. Perhaps he would change his mind. Perhaps...

The doorbell rang, and Harriet's heart leapt.

Brad! It had to be Brad!

She raced from her room, her bare feet flyin
down the hall to the front door. She swung it oper
her face lit with joyous anticipation. 'Brad?' sh
panted.

The man standing on the porch with his back t
her turned slowly round.

Harriet's eyes blinked wide.

But not as wide as the beautiful hazel eyes peerin
closely at her. 'Harriet? Is that you?'

'Graham . . .'

His smile was tentative, then brilliant. 'Goo
God, it *is* you, isn't it?'

She stared back at him, at his elegantly handsom
face, his attractive brown hair, his tall, lean figur
dressed suavely in a smart, if slightly creased, dar
brown suit. While shocked by his sudden appear
ance, Harriet gathered herself quickly, finding cor
fidence when his physical presence and winnin
smile didn't affect her in the slightest. He looked
if anything, better than ever, and yet she fe
nothing, not even that lingering affection she ha
mentioned to Brad.

She returned his smile quite easily, totally relaxin
as this realisation sank in. The only feeling she ha
was a burst of joy for Amanda. Graham ha
pursued her sister all the way back here to Australi
If that wasn't the sign of true love, she didn't kno
what was!

'Of course it's me,' she said lightly. 'Come i
Graham. Come in.' She drew him inside, facing hi
with happy indifference. 'Amanda's gone shoppin
with Mother but she should be home soon. Fanc

a cup of coffee? I was just about to make myself one.'

He gaped at her. 'I can't believe it,' he said. 'You're so different, Harriet. Your hair...your face...your... My God, just look at you!'

Quite unexpectedly he grabbed her hands, holding her arms wide while he looked her over with rather astonishing thoroughness.

'Fantastic! More than fantastic...'

His eyes landed on her breasts, and an unmistakable spark of desire flashed. Startled, Harriet yanked her hands free, laughing away his compliment as she propelled him in the direction of the kitchen. She chatted as she went while her mind fairly whirled, half surprised, half embarrassed by what had just happened. She no longer wanted Graham's desire, in fact found it oddly repellent. The thought bothered her that over the years he might have turned into a bit of a womaniser.

Making coffee was good for a few minutes of keeping Graham at a safe distance, as was her incessant questions about his job, his plane trip from California, his shorter flight up to Coff's Harbour that morning. Graham seemed only too pleased to talk about himself, revealing that a taxi had brought him all the way from the airport, costing him a small fortune. It crossed Harriet's mind that he was trying to impress her with his success.

'So, Harriet?' he said at last. 'Who's the man?'

She was taken aback for a moment, but quickly gathered herself, glancing up from her coffee-mug to smile wryly at him across the kitchen table. 'Man,

Graham? Aren't you jumping to conclusions? I might be *men*.'

His shock delighted the new sense of mischie Brad had instilled in her.

'His name is Brad,' she went on, much t Graham's obvious relief. He had clearly been at loss for words. 'Brad Barrington.' No way was sh going to mention that they were already a past item

Graham's mouth dropped open. 'You mean th famous author?'

Her face was a picture of nonchalance. 'Yes, h does write for a living. Do you know him?'

'Well...n-no,' he blustered. 'Not personally. Bu my God, Harriet, the man's a well-known roué Not the sort of chap a girl like you should get mixec up with.'

She swallowed her fury, adopting instead a typ of casual coldness. 'Really, Graham? Firstly, yo don't know what kind of girl I am now, since yo haven't seen me for years. Not only that, I don' think you're in a position to make judgements. You own life has hardly been conducted abov reproach.'

He had the good grace to blush, then stare morosely down into his coffee. 'So...Amanda tol you about the girl,' he muttered, his answer infuri ating Harriet. His recent infidelity was not his onl black mark. Had he forgotten his shabby treatmen of *her*?

'She told *me*,' she snapped. 'She hasn't told ou parents, the future grandparents of your child!'

His chin jerked up, his eyes appalled.

Harriet sighed. Now she had done it, her ange having opened her big mouth. Though, now sh came to think of it, if anyone had a chance of making Graham see sense, it was herself. 'Yes, Graham,' she went on more calmly, 'Amanda's going to have a baby. Unfortunately, she's afraid you might not believe the baby's yours...'

He dragged in a deep breath before letting it out angrily. 'And she'd be bloody right,' he muttered.

'She swore to me it's yours,' Harriet affirmed. 'And I believe her.'

'Huh!' He picked up the mug and downed the rest of the coffee.

Harriet gritted her teeth. 'Amanda loves you,' she went on with fierce conviction. 'You have to believe that, Graham. People say lots of things they shouldn't when they're hurting, and you hurt her with that girl!'

Graham gave a reluctant nod. 'Yes, I know...'

'Don't you want the baby, Graham?' Even saying the words struck at Harriet's heart. Fancy having to ask if he wanted his baby. Didn't the fool know how lucky he was to be having a child at all?

'I suppose a kid would be nice,' he admitted grudgingly. 'It's just that I've never thought of Amanda as the maternal type.'

'Do you know she's afraid you won't love her as much if her figure changes a bit? You *do* love her, don't you?'

He stared down at the table for a few seconds, then looked up with a sigh. 'I suppose I do, though sometimes I'm not sure...'

'Well, you'd better make up your mind pretty darned quickly, because Amanda will be home soon, and I'm not going to let you hurt my sister as you hurt me. Grow up, Graham! You can't play with people's feelings forever.'

Harriet scrambled to her feet, the chair almost tipping over as she did. She threw Graham a furious look before sweeping up the empty coffee-mugs then marching over to dump them in the sink. 'I need some fresh air,' she announced testily, and strode through to the living area where she flung back the sliding glass doors and stepped out on to the balcony overlooking the valley. She walked over to stand at the railing, dragging in several steadying breaths, annoyed with herself for letting her temper get the better of her.

Graham came up behind her, his hands closing over her shoulders with a gentle, apologetic touch. 'I'm sorry, Harriet,' he murmured, turning her stiff, unrelenting body round to face him. 'You're right. I've been acting like a selfish, immature fool. Of course Amanda and I will get married. And of course I love her.'

'There is no *of course* about it, Graham,' she said irritably. 'Oh, I don't doubt you love her in bed! But do you love her in any other capacity? Do you love her person, her mind?'

'Her mind?' he repeated blankly.

This drew a dry laugh from Harriet. 'She does have one, you know. A very bright one. Nurture it, Graham, as you do all those nubile young students of yours. Nurture it and you might find you have a gem such as you never knew you possessed!'

He was staring at her all the while she was talking as though he had just made the most miraculous discovery. By the time she stopped, a wry smile had curved his attractive mouth to one side. 'I think I've let the real gem already slip through my fingers...Harriet, I——'

'Don't you dare say it,' Harriet hissed. 'Don't you dare!'

He sighed. 'Very well, but you can't expect me not to admire you, Harriet. You've grown into a remarkable woman.' And he leant a soft palm against her cheek.

'It seems I've called at an inopportune time!' came the caustically dry words from behind them.

Harriet froze, then pushed herself away from Graham to behold a cynical-eyed Brad standing, legs apart, arms folded, in the open doorway to the living-room. He looked almost as bad as the first night he had landed on their doorstep. His hair was a mess. His eyes were bloodshot. He still hadn't shaved. And his jeans and flannelette shirt wouldn't have been astray at a jumble sale.

'Brad,' she gulped, her heart fluttering at his unexpected arrival. Oh, dear heaven, what must he think? she groaned silently, glancing over at Graham. Brad wouldn't recognise him and it would look as though she hadn't waited long to get herself another man. And while this probably *shouldn't* bother Brad, with his *c'est la vie* attitude to life and sex, Harriet could see he was looking undeniably peeved.

She stepped forward. 'Brad, it's not what it looks like. This is Graham Banks, come back from America. He——'

Graham chose that unfortunate moment to also step forward, holding out his hand and smiling broadly. 'Mr Barrington,' he enthused. 'Harriet told me about you. I'm very pleased to meet you.'

Brad ignored Graham's hand entirely, setting his stony-faced attention entirely on Harriet. 'You know, Harriet,' he said cuttingly, 'I thought you had some sense, yet here you are, letting this bastard walk back into your life without so much as a by your leave. I might have an unorthodox lifestyle but I've always believed that one should suffer at least a little for one's crimes. There again, I suppose my sense of justice is perhaps as ridiculous as the rest of my emotions. So, Graham, old chap, this is for you!'

And, with that, Brad swung a large balled fist and punched an already startled-looking Graham square in the stomach.

If Harriet had not been so shocked she might have laughed at the comical way Graham's eyes almost popped out of his head, after which he clutched his stomach and sank, gasping, to the wooden decking.

'Be thankful,' Brad added, glaring at Harriet, 'that I didn't hit the bum on the jaw. But I thought you might prefer him with teeth. *Au revoir*, Harriet. I won't wish you every happiness. If you're crazy enough to take this creep back, you don't deserve it! Oh, and by the way, come and collect that bloody useless kitten of yours. I can't take her back to Sydney with me. Pets are not allowed in my unit block. Don't bother to see me out. I know the way and the front door's open. Besides, I think Mr Spick-and-Span there needs some attention.'

He stalked off through the house, leaving Harriet with her mouth open.

'God,' Graham groaned as he struggled to his feet, still holding his stomach.

Harriet turned to help Graham up. 'I'm sorry, Graham,' she said shakily. 'I... I tried to explain, but he wasn't listening.'

'Hmm. You can say that again,' he moaned. 'For a second there I thought Rambo had arrived.' He let out a shuddering sigh and managed to stand fully upright. 'Talk about jealous! Well, Harriet? What are you doing still standing here? Get after the man! Tell him I'm not his rival for your affections.'

'But... but... You don't understand. We broke up. He doesn't love me. He... he...'

Graham laughed. But only briefly. It hurt his stomach. 'Don't give me that rubbish, woman. The man's clearly besotted. And I can't say I blame him.' He gave her a close look between grimaces. 'Or don't you love him?'

She looked so stricken that he sighed again. 'I can see you do,' he murmured wryly. 'Good grief, Harriet, you're not going to let another man get away, are you?'

She stared at him, a whole host of thoughts bombarding her mind, obliterating all her preconceived ideas, replacing them with the most incredible, the most wonderful hopes. He thought Brad loved her... Was *convinced* Brad loved her! What if...?

Quite desperately her mind scanned all that had happened, all that Brad had ever said to her. Not once, she recalled, had he said he *didn't* love her.

Not once. Of course he'd said a lot of things, some downright insulting!

But still... He had certainly acted the part of jealous lover just now...

And it did make sense. Marvellous, mad sense! Brad had been changing even before he had come to live here in Valley's End. She could see that now. He had been throwing off the mantle of bitterness, getting rid of his shallow women, wanting somewhere decent to live, writing more worthwhile stories. His heart had finally been ready to love again, his poor tragic heart. And because when he loved he loved deep and hard, he had been prepared to make the ultimate sacrifice. To send her away, to go away himself, because he loved her!

Oh, if only it were true...

Tears raced to her eyes, but she choked them back, fought them down. This was no time for tears. Tears could come later. 'Do you really think he loves me, Graham?' she asked one last time.

'I'd stake my life on it,' he returned. 'Hell, if Rambo had found me really doing something, like kissing you, I dare say I wouldn't have a life left to stake!'

A huge grin broke over Harriet's face. 'Oh, Graham, I love you,' she burst out, giving him a swift hug and running to get her car keys.

'Hey, watch those loose words,' he called after her. 'A certain person might overhear and think you meant them.'

Harriet was laughing as she raced out, slamming the front door behind her.

CHAPTER TWELVE

BRAD didn't hear her drive up. Or if he did he didn't come out to see who it was.

Despite a stomach sick with nerves Harriet refused to have second thoughts. She got out of the car as soon as she turned off the engine, striding up the front steps on to the veranda where the white kitten was curled up asleep on the rocking-chair.

'Glad to see someone relaxed around here,' she muttered, her hand lifting to knock on the open front door. But millimetres before contacting the wood she hesitated, then with a burst of determination walked right on in.

He was in the lounge-room, thumping books down into a packing crate, muttering away to himself, calling himself a whole litany of names, all uncomplimentary. He didn't see Harriet standing there in the hallway, watching him, her confidence getting a much-needed boost from his manner. Anger meant emotion. *Deep* emotion.

'Brad . . .'

His head snapped up, his face betraying his wretchedness before he could school it into a stony mask. 'If you've come expecting some sort of apology,' he said coldly, 'then you're wasting your time.'

Harriet surprised him by shrugging indifferently and walking into the room. 'I'm sure Graham will recover,' she said. 'Speaking of Graham, though——'

Brad glared at her. 'Good God, you honestly don't expect me to listen while you rave on about the return of your lost love, do you? Just take the cat and go! It's out on the veranda.' He rammed another book down into the box.

Harriet's heart began to pound harder, Brad's seething jealousy fuelling her with more and more hope. But she could see that a straightforward approach might not work. Her original plan had been to declare her own love, then add that she thought he loved her too, but now, all of a sudden, she could see that might not work. If he did love her, and had acted as he'd done because of that love, he would deny it till the cows came home, making his stupid, wonderful sacrifice over and over again.

And so Harriet, honest as the day was long Harriet, decided for the first time in her life to be the most conniving, manipulative female one could ever have imagined. In fact, she was about to make Amanda and her mother look like beginners in the sneaky stakes.

'In a minute. First, I need some advice,' she said with what she hoped was the right amount of confused anguish. 'About Graham...'

She saw his jaw clench, saw the muscles working convulsively at the base of his cheeks.

'What about him?' he asked through gritted teeth.

She came forward, all breathless hesitancy before walking slowly over to the fireplace, leaning one hand on the mantelpiece and staring down into the empty hearth for a few seconds before whirling to face Brad; this whole manoeuvre just so that he could get a good look at what it was Graham had found so attractive. She noticed with a measure of satisfaction that Brad's eyes were glued to her.

'The subject didn't come up yesterday afternoon,' she began carefully, 'but Amanda's left Graham. That's why she's come home.'

'No kidding,' came the dry comment.

'I...I was alone in the house when Graham turned up today, and it gave us the opportunity to sort out some things, and he...well, he...' She let her voice trail away tellingly.

'He what?' Brad growled, blue eyes narrowing.

'He...was rather taken with the new me,' she concluded, not untruthfully.

'"The new me",' Brad mimicked, throwing another book into the crate. 'God, I've created a monster!'

'He wants me back,' she went on with wide-eyed innocence. 'And I...I'm not sure what to do?'

For a second she thought Brad was going to explode. 'And you expect me to advise you?' he snarled. 'Who do you think I am, woman? Dorothy Dix?'

She walked right over to stand next to him. 'I was going to say no, but then he sort of kissed me and——'

Brad's head snapped towards her, his mouth scowling. 'He *sort of* kissed you? How can a man *sort of* kiss you? He either did or he didn't! Which is it?'

She blinked up at him through long, long lashes. 'I suppose he did.'

'How?' he demanded.

'What do you mean, how?'

'What do you think I mean by how? With his mouth open? With his *tongue*?'

She swallowed. Angry, Brad was quite frightening. But wonderful too. He was showing her his feelings with amazing clarity. Why hadn't she seen through him before?

'Yes,' she lied. And held her breath.

He made an explosive, exasperated sound and spun away, striding over to yank some more books from the bookcases.

'Well, Brad?' Harriet prompted with feigned ingenuousness. 'What do you think?'

He glared at her as he stomped back, gripping the books in his hands like weapons. Harriet fancied that any moment they might be hurled at her head. 'What do I think?' The books landed in the crate with a resounding thump. 'I think the bloke's a sheer bastard and that you're a damned fool!'

'You don't think I should sleep with him, then?'

She thought he was going to have apoplexy. '*Sleep* with him?' he repeated, blue eyes blazing. 'You came here to ask me if you should sleep with some other man? My God, Harriet, I thought you were a woman with a degree of sensitivity!'

'But I didn't think you'd mind,' came her supposedly puzzled reply. 'Why should you mind? You're going back to Sydney, aren't you? I doubt you'll be celibate for long once you get there. I'm just taking a leaf out of your book. I'm not in love with Graham any more. I realised that today when he turned up. But he's a very attractive man. I'd forgotten how well he kissed...' she pretended to recall it very fondly. Very fondly indeed '...and, as we discussed, Brad, single partners don't grow on trees around Valley's End. Of course I'd rather have you as my lover but since you won't be here...'

She saw the wheels turning in his mind as he examined his alternatives. His acting wasn't bad either, once his decision had been made. His face took on a mildly exasperated, blasé expression while he moved slowly towards her. 'Now, look, Harriet, don't do anything hasty. If all this comes down to your need of a lover, then perhaps we could come to an arrangement. You could come back to Sydney to teach and we could——'

'Oh, no, Brad, I wouldn't want to be beholden to you. Besides, you have your rules. No emotional involvement.'

He stopped before her, his smile cool and confident as his hands reached out to cradle her face. 'I think that after this little episode I'm convinced you don't love me, Harriet,' he drawled, his head bending.

'But I wasn't referring to me, Brad,' she murmured just before his mouth met hers.

His hands froze around her face, his head slowly lifting to stare down at her.

'I know you love me,' she stated with apparent calm. Underneath she was like jelly.

He sucked in a startled breath, his hands dropping from her face as if he'd been stung by a scorpion. But he quickly gathered his wits, stepping back from her and putting on a drily amused expression. 'Whatever gave you such a——?'

'Please don't deny it,' she cut in frantically, her pretence gone, her real emotions surfacing with all their accompanying desperation. 'Because I love you too. I love you so much I'd rather die than lose you...' A lump had gathered in her throat, making her voice sound horribly strangled. 'I know you think you're doing the noble thing, pretending you don't love me, letting me be free to find some man who could give me a baby. But Brad...darling...' She came forward, dashing away the threatening tears before slipping her arms up around his neck, holding on to him for dear life. 'There is more to life than having babies. Much more.'

He was looking down at her with a mixture of wonderment and frustration in his eyes. 'Harriet...sweetheart...you don't understand. You're right about my loving you. I do. Terribly. But I——'

'You *do*?' she gasped, her heart turning over.

'Yes, but——'

'Then there are no buts,' she broke in, the wave of relief overflowing into a flood of wild determination. 'Can't you see that? We love each other and nothing is going to keep us apart again. Nothing. We'll be happy together, Brad. Really happy. I'll help you with your new book, doing research, checking your manuscript, anything! I'll even come to Sydney with you if that's what you want. Only please, if you love me, don't send me away again...'

Her voice faltered, her eyes filling. 'Can't you see,' she went on brokenly, 'that if you leave me I won't have children, anyway? You've spoilt me for any other man. Completely spoilt me... No other man will ever measure up. It's *you* I love, *you* I want, *you* I need!'

For a moment she was sure Brad was going to cry, but instead he caught her to him, hugging her so tightly that all the breath was squeezed out of her. 'Oh, Harriet,' he cried. 'Wonderful, wonderful Harriet!' Suddenly he drew back, a slight frown on his face. 'What about dear old Graham?'

Harriet looked sheepish.

Brad grinned. 'You were lying, you little devil, weren't you?'

'Lying my teeth out,' she admitted. 'Graham came to get Amanda, not me. I was trying to make you jealous, to goad you into betraying your love for me. And you did.'

'Why, you...!' He shook her, then dragged her against him, kissing her with an indescribable hunger. 'God, you've no idea what I went through when I saw him holding you, touching you. I wanted to tear him limb from limb.'

Harriet giggled. 'You controlled yourself quite well, then, didn't you? Only one itsy-bitsy little punch! Poor Graham, did you see his face crumple?'

'Poor Graham indeed!' Brad humphed. 'I think that's one thing you weren't lying about. He was coming on to you, wasn't he?'

'Of course not.' There were times when a small white lie was wise. 'He's in love with Amanda.

Now, confess, why did you come to the house? I wasn't just to tell me to take the kitten, was it?'

'No...' He led her over to their favourite arm chair and settled into it, drawing her on to his lap 'When I saw you yesterday afternoon, being s sweet to that vampire of a sister of yours, I wa thrown into total despair. I admired and wante you so much. Not just in bed. I wanted you in m life...forever. I didn't sleep a wink last night fo thinking about you, loving you, wanting you, so i the end I got out of bed and started making phon calls.'

'Phone calls?' Harriet repeated, puzzled. Wher on earth was this leading?

'Yes, phone calls! Scores of them. Thank the lore I'm rich, though I might have to toss off anothe sexy bestseller to cover my phone bill. Do you knov how hard it is to track down medical records an specialists on a public holiday? But, as they say i the classics, where there's a will there's a way. An brother, did I have *will*!'

'Brad, darling, you certainly write a lot mor simply than you talk. Give it to me in a nutshell.

'In a nutshell?' He grinned down at her. 'Yo don't realise it but that's almost a pun, con sidering——'

'*Brad!*'

'It's reversible!' he burst out, a wide grin on hi face. 'My vasectomy, that is. Can you believe it There's this doctor, a specialist in micro-surgery who's quite confident he can have me disgustingl potent in no time. So you see, Harriet? We *ca* have a baby, eventually. That was what I wa

coming to tell you today.' He shrugged, a look of
wry foolishness on his face. 'But when I saw you
with lover-boy, I guess I went off at a tangent...'

Harriet could hardly contain the joy in her heart.
It was the ultimate, the most fantastic news. Like
a miracle! As if God had smiled on them with all
his love and mercy! She wanted to say something,
to put into words what she was feeling. But she
couldn't. All she could do was lay her head on
Brad's chest and sigh his name.

Oh, how she loved this man. He was her pro-
tector, her prince, her knight in shining armour,
her...

Her head shot up, her expression worried.

'What now?' he asked, frowning.

'You know, if there are to be kiddies I'm afraid
you'll have to marry me. I'm an old-fashioned girl,
remember?'

A devilish light sparkled in his wicked blue eyes.
'Married! Now that's taking things a bit far, don't
you think? I mean...my fans wouldn't be too happy
with bad Brad Barrington taking a wife.' He collapsed into hysterical laughter as she started tickling
him. 'Mercy mercy,' he squawked. 'I give in. I'll
marry you. Mercy...'

'Didn't I tell you, Raymond, that they might fall
in love?' Julia pronounced with a self-satisfied
smirk. 'Right from the start I said, "Now, doesn't
he sound like a suitable husband for our Harriet?"!'

Harriet gave Brad a surreptitious poke in the ribs
from where they were sitting jammed together on
the chesterfield. 'I'll bet you didn't know *that*,' she

whispered, 'when you showed up here for dinne
looking like a vagrant.'

'No fear,' he muttered back. 'I would have ru
a mile.'

'What are you two whispering about?' Julia sai
impatiently.

'Just wedding plans, Mother.'

'Well, there's one person who won't be surprise
by your news,' Julia announced smugly. 'Old Mr
Gallagher. She was out pottering in her garden whe
we drove past from Coff's Harbour earlier today
so I stopped for a little chat, thinking she might b
lonely. Apparently, though, she's been kept quit
busy writing some book on cats you suggested t
her, Brad. Anyway, she didn't stop raving abou
how kind you both have been to her, and how she'
never seen a couple so obviously in love. She wa
laughing over how coy you've both been, and t
be truthful, Harriet, I have to agree with her.
mean, you could have let us in on things a bit more
instead of saying that you and Brad were "just goo
friends". Don't you agree, Raymond?'

Raymond bestowed a soothing smile on his wife
'Now, Julia, young people these days have a dif
ferent attitude to such matters from the one we had
Everything is much more casual. Be grateful they'r
getting married at all, I say.'

'Raymond!'

'Well, just look at Graham and Amanda,' h
retorted. 'OK, so they're getting married now, bu
they've been living together for four years and al
ready expecting a baby.'

'Expecting a baby?' Brad repeated, giving Harriet a reproving look. 'Forget that little piece of news, did you?'

'Thought it a wise decision at the time,' she mumbled.

'And I suppose it was you who engineered Graham and Amanda leaving for America before we drove home today,' he went on, but with a teasing light in his eyes.

'I did think it best...'

Harriet looked up to find her parents making a tactical retreat from the room, leaving them alone.

'And I think you talk too much,' Brad finished. And kissed her.

After the third kiss, they settled into a relaxed huddle.

'Tell me,' Harriet murmured. 'When *did* you fall in love with me?'

'Difficult to say,' he sighed. 'I first realised I was in trouble when you were helping me pack away my books and you said, "me, too".'

She blinked up at him in astonishment, recalling that that was the moment when he had gone green around the gills and she'd thought he was having a heart attack.

'Oddly enough, it was something Helen used to say all the time,' he elaborated. 'I looked up, half expecting to see her standing there, but it was you, Harriet. And all of a sudden it was as if someone had punched me in the stomach. I was panic-stricken. I thought, hell, this isn't some hard-nosed female, this is a warm, feeling woman. What if I'm falling in love with her? And, worse, what if she

falls in love with me? I knew I should have cut ou
relationship off then and there, but I kept kiddin
myself I could keep it all in check. But I was playin
with fire, wasn't I, my little incendiary rocket?' H
gave her a kiss on the cheek, then her ear, then he
throat, then...

She pushed him away, frowning. 'You mean
remind you of your wife?' she asked, worried.

'Not at all. Other than that particular phrase yo
used, you're not even remotely like Helen. She wa
a sweet girl, and I loved her dearly, but lookin
back she was just that. A girl...as I was a boy
Perhaps that was why I couldn't cope with he
death. I went berserk, cutting myself off from m
family with my outrageous behaviour, treatin
women as little better than objects for my own ends
putting on this ghastly sophisticated act to a worl
I thought was too painful to endure.'

'But that wasn't the real you, Brad,' she soothed
'You showed the real you to me. Kind, generous
loving...'

'That's because I had fallen in love with you
Harriet, you with your endearing honesty, you
genuine warmth, your smouldering sexuality. An
yes...your chip on your shoulder. I could empathis
with that...'

'My smouldering sexuality?' she repeate
dazedly.

'You don't agree?'

'Well, no...I always thought of myself as
fraction cold before you brought me out of m
shell.' But even as she denied it she suspected Bra
was right. Underneath, she had always been highl

sexed. That was what had made her seeming lack of attractiveness to the opposite sex such a torment. Her cold aloofness had been a façade to hide the frustration. Yet the façade had only perpetuated the vicious circle, making males turn away from her even more.

'It was there right from the start, Harriet,' Brad whispered into her ear. 'In your eyes.' Which of course it had been. She hadn't been able to take her eyes off him that first night at dinner. 'And might I ask you the same question?' he retaliated. 'When did you fall in love with me?'

'I think...perhaps...when I watched you being interviewed on television. At least, that was when the seed was sown. It only needed you in the flesh to burst into life.'

He pulled her even closer, if that was possible. 'My darling Harriet, you can have all of me in the flesh you like.' His hand started roving under the jumper.

'Stop being naughty!' she reprimanded, but she didn't strike his hand away.

'You like me naughty.'

'I like you any way,' she laughed, her ribs being ticklish.

'Let's go back to my place?'

'All right,' she agreed eagerly.

They rose and made their way to the front door. 'I'm taking Harriet out for dinner, folks,' Brad called. 'Don't wait up!'

Julia materialised in the foyer, all smiles. 'How nice. Well, have a good time, dears. Oh, Harriet, could you spare just a second or two before you go?'

Harriet raised her eyebrows at Brad but followed her mother down the hall. 'Yes?'

Her mother leant forward like a conspirator. 'I do realise you're a grown woman, Harriet,' she whispered, 'but I feel I have to say something. I mean...you've always been a bit...naïve...where men are concerned, and a man like Brad... Well they can prove quite difficult to handle. They don't always like to wait till the wedding night...'

Harriet must have looked odd as she battled to control a fit of the giggles.

'Thank you, Mother,' she said with quivering lips and chin, 'but I think I can manage Brad all right. He's very kind and considerate, and he only wants what I want.'

Julia relaxed into a smile. 'That's a comfort to know. Oh, I think your father wanted to say something to you as well. He's in the study. I'll keep Brad entertained while he's waiting.'

Harriet opened the study door with a sense of curiosity. She could not recall the last time her father had asked to speak to her privately.

Raymond looked up from where he was sitting behind his desk. 'Ah, Harriet! Come in, my dear, come in.'

'I can't stay, Father. Brad and I are just off to dinner.'

'A celebratory dinner, eh? Splendid idea. Well, I won't keep you. I just wanted to say—and for Pete's sake don't repeat this to your mother, or Amanda—but between my two prospective sons-in-law, I think you got the better catch, by far!' He beamed at Harriet, then actually stood up to come round and give her a kiss. Harriet stood there, astonished. 'I've been very worried about you, my dear. Very worried. I've never been good at understanding women. Never. But I can see you've worked your problems all out by yourself and I think it's splendid. Just splendid!' And he actually hugged her!

Harriet left the room quite speechless, wandering back down to the foyer in a daze.

'Are you all right, Harriet?' Brad asked with a frown.

She looked up at him and her equally frowning mother, then her face broke out into the widest smile.

'Perfectly all right.'

She surprised her mother with an exuberant kiss before slipping an arm through Brad's.

'Ready?' he asked with a grin.

'Always,' she grinned back.

She tightened her grip on his arm and let him lead her outside, thinking as she went that if only Brad could make up with his parents then her happiness would be complete. He was their only son, he had told her, having two married sisters, and their estrangement had lasted for far too long, she believed.

Brad helped her into the passenger seat of the Porsche before striding round to climb in behind the driver's wheel, where he cast her a troubled look. 'Now what is going on in that devious mind of yours, Harriet? I smell trouble.'

'Not at all, darling. Not at all.'

'Oho! I definitely smell trouble when you start calling me darling like that!'

'I was merely thinking that, when we get back to your place, it would be nice if you made one more phone call...to your parents.'

His eyebrows almost hit the roof of the car, his sigh both exasperated and resigned. 'I knew it!'

'Knew what?' she asked, all wide-eyed and innocent.

'That you were a bossy-boots! The moment I laid eyes on you I said, Now that woman is definitely a bossy-boots. She——'

Harriet silenced him the only way she could think of. With her lips. They were still kissing when the little kitten woke up on the back seat and miaowed plaintively.

'Good grief!' Brad exclaimed, reeling away from Harriet's mouth. 'That damned cat almost gave me a heart attack. I'd forgotten we'd brought her with us.'

Harriet scooped the little bundle of fur into her lap. 'Well, we couldn't leave her alone up at your place for too long, could we, Brigit, sweetie?' she crooned.

The kitten settled into Harriet's lap under her rhythmic stroking, all contentment and purrs.

'Don't go thinking that animal's going to sleep on our bed!' he warned.

'Of course not, darling.'

Brad was shaking his head as he started the engine. 'And when you start saying "Of course not, darling", I smell double trouble,' he growled.

'Now, Brad, you make me sound like some sort of shrew.'

'Hmm.' His sideways glance was so wickedly sexy that Harriet's heart leapt.

'What on earth are you thinking?' she gasped.

He reproduced the same innocent expression she had adopted earlier.

'Brad Barrington, what *are* you thinking?'

'Just recalling my favourite Shakespearian play,' he tossed off.

'*The Taming of the Shrew*?' she suggested drily.

'Heck, no!'

'What, then?'

'*As You Like It*.'

'*As You Like It*?' she repeated, surprised.

His grin was more than wicked. 'And I like it, Harriet. I like it a lot.'

They were both laughing as the car shot up the road.

Relive the romance...
Harlequin®is proud to bring you

A new collection of three complete novels every
month. By the most requested authors, featuring
the most requested themes.

Available in October:

DREAMSCAPE

They're falling under a spell!
But is it love—or magic?

Three complete novels in one special collection:

GHOST OF A CHANCE by Jayne Ann Krentz
BEWITCHING HOUR by Anne Stuart
REMEMBER ME by Bobby Hutchinson

Available wherever Harlequin books are sold.

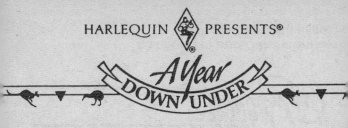

HARLEQUIN 💎 PRESENTS®

A Year
DOWN UNDER

In 1993, Harlequin Presents celebrates the land down under. In October, let us take you to rural New Zealand in WINTER OF DREAMS by Susan Napier, Harlequin Presents # 1595.

Olivia Marlow never wants to see Jordan Pendragon again—their first meeting had been a humiliating experience. The sexy New Zealander had rejected her then, but now he seems determined to pursue her. Olivia knows she must tread carefully—she has something to hide. But then, it's equally obvious that Jordan has his own secret....

Share the adventure—and the romance—of A Year Down Under!

Available this month in
A YEAR DOWN UNDER

AND THEN CAME MORNING
by Daphne Clair
Harlequin Presents # 1586
Available wherever Harlequin books are sold.